To Rachel New[...]
and FMF part[...]
& God's blessings,

Terry Umpherson

ACROSS A BROKEN SKY

ACROSS A BROKEN SKY

▼

Terry Umphenour

Writer's Showcase
New York   Lincoln   Shanghai

Across a Broken Sky

All Rights Reserved © 2001 by Terry Umphenour

No part of this book may be reproduced or transmitted in any form or by any means, graphic, electronic, or mechanical, including photocopying, recording, taping, or by any information storage retrieval system, without the written permission of the publisher.

Writer's Showcase
an imprint of iUniverse, Inc.

For information address:
iUniverse
2021 Pine Lake Road, Suite 100
Lincoln, NE 68512
www.iuniverse.com

ISBN: 0-595-17949-5

Printed in the United States of America

This book is dedicated to my dearest daughters, Olga and Roksana, and to the many young people whose spirits make Karina come alive.

Epigraph

Climb the highest mountaintops,
And dive the deepest of the seas.
Sail high up into the heavens,
And you may drift upon the breeze.

Though the mysteries of the forest,
May lie hidden from your sight,
And clouds of darkness are prevailing,
You will coast safely through the night.

Reach down deep within your heart,
And accomplish every hidden goal.
Help those who are less fortunate,
And soothe the tortures of the soul.

For to walk the path less traveled,
May take you far away from home.
Seek first to fulfill the dreams of others,
And you will never walk alone.

-author attribution

Chapter 1

▼

Nightmares

Falling! Karina had a horrible feeling, as if the bottom had dropped out from underneath her. Then, just as suddenly, she felt like a giant was sitting on her chest. She tried to tug her seat belt tighter, panic in her every movement. Small, frantic fingers struggled with the obstinate buckle as the little four-seat private plane bounced around in the thunderstorm.

In her heart, Karina knew this was not a normal situation. Through brilliant lightning flashes that provided eerie illumination, she observed her father struggling for control. Mother was helping him.

Strange, Mother never helped Father fly. Russian fighter pilots didn't need help, so this must be an extreme emergency, Karina thought. Dimly through the howling wind, pounding rain, and explosive thunder, she heard her father give the order to get ready.

"Mother, what's happening?" she asked, her young voice trembling.

"The storm's giving us a thrill, just like a rollercoaster, up and down," her mother shouted over a peal of thunder, crawling back over the front seat to sit beside her. "Cover up with pillows. They'll protect against these hard seats."

Her mother's relaxed manner, tucking pillows snuggly in around her, somewhat reassured Karina, almost like being in her own bed at home. If only the plane would stop cavorting up and down before she lost her dinner. "Mother, is everything okay? I'm frightened!"

"All's well. It's only a storm. Father will take care of us."

Her mother's comforting smile put Karina at ease. That was how it always was. When she scraped her knees, banged her head, or presented the direst catastrophe, her mother would take the pain away with assurances that all would be well in its own time. Nothing ever ruffled her mother, not even last year when Karina fell from that nasty, spirited pony and broke her arm during her own birthday party. Pain and fear melted away as her mother's, tender arms gathered her up, and those magical words brushed aside her worries. Yet, deep inside, Karina knew this was different.

Suddenly, a bright flash lit up the entire world. The right wing dropped sharply, and the plane began to spiral downward, like an awkward child's cartwheel. In that fleeting second, while lightening engulfed them, Karina saw the white-capped mountaintops peaking at what seemed to be an arm's length away.

"Mother!" she screamed.

"Don't worry, darling. Everything will be all right in its own time."

More pillows piled on top of her. Karina could see nothing. Her stomach was in her mouth, spinning around and around. Only her mother's voice filtered through. All else seemed distant now, even the howling wind and crashing thunder.

Yet, real fear mounted. She gasped short, rapid breaths through the soft pillow while her heart pounded in her ears and her sweaty hands searched the billowy folds in a desperate search for her mother. A heavy weight pressed against her, weighing her down, holding her immobile. Only her feet, tapping against the seat in front of her as if they had a life of their own, protruded beneath the burden pressing down upon her.

The world grew dark. The plane's screaming engine rose to a fevered pitch, only to be cut short by screeching metal rivets as they gave way to a frigid blast of cold, wet air. Falling, freezing, cold, wet...

"Mother!"

* * *

Karina struggled through the damp sheets that snaked around her, restraining her every movement. At first she didn't know where she was. Her eyes focused on the curved metal roof, only inches above her head, and her mind slowly brushed away the last cobwebs of her nightmare. Had she screamed out loud, or was it that terrible scream that lurked inside her head, waiting for her guard to drop in sleep?

Squinting, she peered at the top bunk across from her. Her roommate's dark form did not stir. The only visible movement was the gentle rise and fall of slumber. No, the scream must have been in her head, or surely Jessica would have been roused from her sleep.

Amazement quickly turned to anger. The scream was a part of her she could not forget. It had repeated itself, night after endless night, for over six years. Maybe she didn't want it to end. After all, it was the only memory she had left of her mother's gentle voice.

Unwrapping herself from the constricting sheets, Karina inched downward, carefully placing her bare feet onto the smooth cement floor beneath her. She was soaking wet again. Her head ached and her mouth felt as dry as cotton.

Sliding friction from her slow, cautious descent had hiked her nightshirt upward, exposing unsightly scars on her legs where sharp bone had ripped gashes below her right knee all the way down to her slender ankle. Damage to the left leg was not so obvious. A quarter-sized, white scar where her fractured femur had punched upward through the middle of her thigh was all that remained visible.

Karina tiptoed slowly to the door. No need to wake anyone else after the day they had just finished. Morning would come soon enough. She pushed the heavy wooden door open and stepped into cool night air. The breeze gently lifted her shoulder-length reddish brown hair, like the tail of an ancient Chinese kite.

Drifting away from the Quonset hut that she had called home for the past month, Karina found herself facing the instrument of her greatest fear. Sitting there, directly in front of her on the grass next to the hut, was a small two-seat ultralight airplane. Its 32-foot wingspan made it look like a blue albatross waiting to reach for the heavens above.

Shaking slightly, Karina unlatched the canopy door, raised it above her head, and quietly lifted herself into the front seat. The plane lowered to the ground and rested on its nose wheel.

With the instrument panel aglow from soft moonlight flooding in around her, Karina's mind wandered over the events that had delivered her here to Mitchum Field. It seemed like a lifetime had passed since the accident—a lifetime occurring in another place at the outer edge of her memory. Mitchum Field, New York, was half a world away from her beloved homeland, Kyrgyzstan.

After almost six months in a rehabilitation hospital and seven surgeries, Karina was finally released to her Aunt Roksana. Depressed and unwilling to accept her parents' deaths, she had at first refused to believe what her heart knew was true. Her eight-year-old mind made believe that her mother and father were still in the hospital, healing slowly from horrible wounds that just needed time to mend.

Then, when such thoughts no longer gave her comfort, anger set in, anger that overcame her, taking control of every action, every harsh word, and every moment. She became sulky and depressed. Refusing to eat and unable to sleep because of the persistent nightmares, Karina grew too difficult for Aunt Roksana to manage. So, off to America she was sent to an aunt and uncle from her mother's side of the family, an older couple she never even knew existed.

Karina placed her hand on the control stick in front of her. Moving it from left to right against her legs raised or lowered the wings' ailerons, which controlled the airplane's turns while in flight. However, here on the ground, sitting still, the moves were useless.

Useless, Karina thought. *Yes, that describes my life: useless.* Living in America had not been so awful at first. America was truly the land of plenty. But living with an aunt and uncle who were old enough to be her grandparents did not sit well with Karina. She had been seeking the excitement that her father always brought to any event and her mother's easygoing, friendly manner. What she got were caring people who thought strict discipline and routine could replace the domineering anger that possessed her.

Well, it didn't work, at least not in the long run. Oh, yeah, Karina settled down for a while, dociled by rigid routine and unrelenting rules that guided her through each day.

But, as time passed and she grew older, rules and routine failed to replace the nightmares. They continued, and with increasing age, she became more rebellious. First, battles were only words, constant arguments over nothing. Arguments transformed into more substantial resistance: sneaking out at night, skipping school, and running away. Finally, the worst, she was caught shoplifting a sweater and cap—the required bounty for membership in an elite peer social group.

The juvenile court judge had given fourteen-year-old Karina a difficult choice: "Although this is your first offense, I am concerned about where your behavior is leading, so I'm offering you two options. You can either spend the next two years in juvenile detention, or you can participate in an alternative education program centered on building and flying ultralight airplanes."

At first Karina couldn't believe her ears. Two years of confinement was an eternity. She couldn't stand being locked away for that long. But flying? Was the judge crazy? Surely he knew her history. Wasn't there something in the American justice system that prohibited cruel and unusual punishment?

Peering through the front windshield of the ultralight, Karina felt as if she was speeding down the grass runway. She pulled hard on the brake handle attached to the control stick, but in her mind, the plane rolled faster and faster. So did her thoughts, the terrible fight and cruel words she'd had for her aunt and uncle. The tears, pleading and begging the judge still brought her shame every time she remembered her court appearance.

Now, here she was. Karina noticed her knuckles, white from her death grip on the control stick, and her legs, trembling with fatigue from constant pressure on the rudder pedals.

"What's wrong with me?" she cried out.

With a deep sigh, Karina forced herself to release her hold on the control stick and hoisted herself from the cockpit. Once again, her bare feet were on solid ground. The fragrant, pine-scented wind rushed cool and damp against her nightshirt. Over her shoulder, she noticed the first glimmer of sunrise highlighting the hills beyond, the dawn of another day.

"Please," she whispered. "Let the wind blow hard today. Let it rain."

Today, it was her turn to start flight training. Today, she would be sitting at the controls of the very ultralight she had just departed. Today was the day she had feared since coming to Mitchum Field.

"God, give me strength," she prayed and turned quietly toward the hut. She crept silently into her room.

Jessica snored softly, arms wrapped around her pillow as if it was a teddy bear. Karina slipped past the sleeping girl and climbed into bed. She was cold. Her nightshirt, wet from sweat and the damp night air, chilled her to the bone. She pulled the sheets over her head and curled into a tight ball, knees close to her chin. Slowly, Karina warmed and the world began to drift away. Gradually, her eyelids fluttered and closed.

Chapter 2

Flight Day

"Hey, sleepyhead, you better get a move on or you'll miss breakfast." Jessica gently shook Karina. "You know Martin doesn't like anyone skipping meals on flight day."

"Flight day? Oh, no! Tell him I'm sick in bed." Bright sunlight streaming in through the Quonset hut window replaced hazy sleep. Karina pulled the sheets tightly up over her head. After all, she was still soaking wet. Maybe they would think she had a fever. "My head is killing me, and I'm drenched with sweat. I must have a fever or something."

Jessica fastened the snaps on her blue flight suit and reached for a hairbrush. "Won't work. Everyone knows you wake up in a sweat with a headache more mornings than not. Besides, you get to fly today. Aren't you excited?"

"I'm not sure I'd go right to excited," Karina said. She shoved the covers aside, sat up and swung her legs over the edge of the bed. Jessica was right. Everyone knew about her nightmares. "Terrified, maybe, or just plain scared stiff."

Karina noticed Jessica's gaze fixed upon her, watching as she lowered herself carefully from her bunk and grabbed a towel and washcloth from her dressing table. The two girls were friends, but Karina had always kept the conversation light and seldom talked about herself. She had no desire to reveal anything to the kids that might make her vulnerable. After all, placing trust in so-called friends was what had landed her at Blue Horizons. Inside, Karina felt a special closeness to her roommate but not close enough to divulge secrets from her past.

"What are you doing here, Karina? I mean, you hate even the thought of flying. You've passed up every opportunity for riding in the planes, much less flying them. Are you afraid we didn't put them together right?"

Karina looked at the petite, auburn-haired girl standing across from her. "It's not how they're put together that worries me. It's how they'll hold together when they hit the ground."

She grabbed her bathroom kit and headed into the shower, reflecting on the events that had occurred since her arrival at the small ultralight airfield she now called home. Every day since her arrival at the beginning of March, they had been building ultralight airplanes from kits. Now it was mid-April, and they had completed the project's construction phase. Under the direction of experienced staff, the kids had built six airplanes. Two were double-seat Challenger II training airplanes and four were single-seat Challenger ultralights.

The planes had arrived in kit form, 49 percent finished, but completion still required much time and effort. Holes had to be drilled, rivets inserted, and wings and tail sections assembled. Then, sailcloth had to be glued to the wings and the engine assembly mounted. Challenger airplanes were called "pushers" because their engines were mounted behind the cockpit. Finally, the planes were painted and given identifying names.

Karina turned on the shower, slipped out of her nightshirt and panties, and tested the water by sticking her foot into the steaming spray. It felt just right. She moved into the shower and let its warm stream engulf her. Yet, she shivered from within. She had enjoyed the building process, and she had to admit, there were times when being at Blue Horizons wasn't so bad. If only she didn't have to get into the stupid planes. On the runway they looked beautiful, but could she force herself to sit in one as it left the security of the ground?

* * *

Dressed in white T-shirt, blue shorts, tennis shoes, and a blue set of coveralls that served as a flight suit at Blue Horizons, Karina entered the mess hall. She went through the line and collected pancakes, hash brown potatoes, toast, and orange juice before selecting a seat at the far end of the hall. She wanted to be alone. As the time for climbing into that ultralight drew closer, she didn't want to talk to anyone. She didn't know what to say. Her court records were sealed, so only the lead instructor, Martin Campbell, knew about her accident. Most of the students at the school were puzzled by her fear of flying. Why, she even broke out in a sweat during classes on avionics—how the airplane was controlled in flight.

"Karina, better hurry. Briefing is in Classroom 3 at precisely eight-thirty. Don't be late." Martin's crisp business-like voice startled her out of her reverie.

He was a short man, not much taller than her five feet, four inches. His slight stature, bushy moustache, grayish-white hair, and dark-rimmed glasses gave one the impression of an old English professor. But his voice always carried an air of authority, and when it came to flying, there was no one better. He could take off and land in half a football field, zoom up into the heavens, or coast along on slow flight better than seemed humanly possible. No one messed around with Martin. Talking back or refusing his commands was certainly out of the question.

"I'll be on time, sir." She gulped down the last of her orange juice.

Carrying her dishes to the return counter, Karina surveyed the rest of her classmates sitting at two long tables excitedly discussing the day's upcoming activity with hints of anxiety surfacing on overemphasized words. They were a strange lot, all sent here by anxious parents at their wits' end or, like Karina, under the direction of the court. Seven boys and eight girls, between fourteen and sixteen years of age, including Karina, called Blue Horizons home. She barely knew them, even though she'd been living and working with them every day since early March.

Karina dumped her trash into the proper container and shoved her dishes through the window to dishwashers waiting inside the small, efficient kitchen. The group of her classmates was beginning to break up. Still, they reminded her of the events that had landed her at Blue Horizons. It had been a terrible day right from the beginning. An argument with her aunt led to her uncle grounding her for two weeks, which meant she would miss the "big one," the Spring Festival Dance. This led to more yelling on her part and a door slamming departure that was sure to cause her more grief when she returned home.

At school, things quickly went from bad to worse. She received a week's detention for cheating on a French test, which was a really stupid test in a really stupid class. The ensuing argument with her guidance counselor earned her a second week's detention for what was termed "insubordination." Why did she have to take French? She spoke fluent Russian, and it wasn't as if she was going to France in the near future anyway.

Then, things really got bad. She had been trying to get acceptance from the high-society crowd at school that had somehow decided her European heritage was a plus. All she had to do was shoplift a couple of items from the mall. It would be easy. The girls would distract the sales staff. But, had anyone thought about hidden cameras? No!

"Ouch!" The floor hit her before she knew what was happening. She had stepped on a squished melon slice and landed soundly on her behind—served her right for walking and daydreaming at the same time. Embarrassed, Karina carefully picked herself up and gathered her scattered dishes. She could feel the group staring at her; heard their sudden silence.

"You okay? Here, let me help you." Joe Wendell reached down and gave her a hand. "You landed pretty hard. Penny for your thoughts."

"Thanks." Karina's embarrassment changed to delight. She couldn't believe her luck. Ever since Joe arrived last week, she had been trying to get his attention. "But my thoughts aren't worth a penny. You'd be getting gypped." She rubbed her fanny. "Guess I'd better be more careful."

"Yep," he agreed, opening the mess hall door. "Won't be much fun sitting on a bruised rear for two hours in flight. Those seats aren't designed for comfort."

It wasn't much of a conversation, but time was short. Together, they strolled to the classroom. Inside, students were getting organized and turning their attention to Martin. Karina picked a seat next to Jessica and was disappointed when Joe chose to sit in the front row on the opposite side of the room.

Sitting in class and listening to the day's weather forecast seemed boring. Karina was distracted. Her eyes continually glanced in Joe's direction. She couldn't get him from her mind. Somehow wind speed, chances of precipitation, and daytime temperatures didn't seem important. She noted the data onto her kneeboard, a small clipboard with paper strapped to her right thigh.

Martin was lecturing. "The primary radio frequency will be channel "C" for air-to-ground communication. Set intercoms on channel "A" for pilot-to-instructor communications. Landing and takeoff patterns will be east to west with clockwise rotation. Pattern altitude is 1800-feet mean sea level. Karina! Are you getting all of this?"

"Yes, sir!" Her head jerked up, and she made a mental note to ask Jessica for anything she had missed. Her heart was racing. Did Martin know what she was really thinking? Could he be reading her mind? Was it that obvious? She shook the pleasantry of Joe's conversation from her mind in time to hear Martin's next words.

"Right, then. Jessica, you'll fly with Sally in *Blue Bird*, and Karina will fly with me in *Jet Stream*."

Her stomach did flip-flops. "Sir, do you mean now? I thought we weren't supposed to fly until after lunch."

Martin walked over and stood directly in front of her. "I believe in this morning's briefing, I made it perfectly clear that we would be reversing our normal schedule because clouds will be rolling in around noon." He firmly placed his hand on her shoulder. "Flying is serious business, Karina. It can be extremely rewarding, but mistakes can be unforgiving. You should know that."

Karina's head dropped, and she nodded agreement. "Sorry."

"It's history now. You and Jessica go and get your gear." He turned to the rest of the group. "Paul, Sarah, you preflight *Blue Bird*. Jeff, Katie, you preflight *Jet Stream*. The rest of you are on maintenance detail and ground support. Shake a leg, people."

Without further words, Martin marched briskly from the classroom and headed in the direction of the flight ready room.

"Well," Jessica said, offering Karina her kneeboard. "Guess this is it. You okay? You're as white as a ghost."

Karina quickly jotted down the information she had missed. "Let's go before I lose my nerve." She pushed her way through the rest of the kids, Jessica hot on her heels. Karina knew that if she didn't move quickly, she would break down and cry right in front of everyone.

* * *

Karina stood in front of *Jet Stream,* watching the preflight operations. Before every flight, a ground team preflighted the ultralight while the pilot looked on. Then, the pilot did the very same thing. Every rivet, locking pin, and moveable part of the plane was checked and rechecked before and after each flight. Her sweaty hands trembled, checking the rudder for ease of movement. She knew Martin was watching closely, waiting for her to make a mistake, any mistake. He didn't do it to reprimand her, but it made her angry anyway. She didn't want to be here. She detested the very thought of flying.

"Everything ready?" Martin asked as Karina finished her inspection. He had already put on his helmet and was checking out the ground crew's performance.

"She's flight ready," Karina said, and they both climbed into the little airplane. This was a trick because the "skin" of the plane was sailcloth. Putting too much pressure on it anywhere could lead to a tear.

Karina sat in front. Martin, as flight instructor, sat in the back seat. Each seat possessed a seat belt and shoulder harness designed to keep the occupant from bouncing up and hitting the canopy during any sudden drop in altitude. The plane had dual controls and could be flown from either the front or back seat. An intercom set, controlled from the helmet, linked Karina to Martin. Turning the knob changed the intercom into a two-way radio that allowed air-to-ground communication. A full instrument panel gave Karina important information needed for the coming flight—airspeed, altitude, center of gravity, and artificial horizon, among others.

"Radio check. Karina, do you copy?" Martin's voice rang through her headset into her ears.

"Loud and clear," she said.

"Okay, start her up. Remember to shout 'clear' before turning the prop. We'll just taxi up and down the field for now."

Karina put the key into the ignition, shouted 'clear' as required, and turned the key. The engine's roar startled her. She would have jumped and hit her head if it had not been for the restraining belts holding her tight, locking her into the seat.

For the better part of twenty minutes, she taxied the ultralight up and down the grass runway, going faster and faster with each run. Martin reminded her not to go faster than 35-miles per hour or the ultralight might leave the ground. Takeoff speed with two people aboard was 40-miles per hour. Martin didn't need to worry; she wasn't about to leave the ground any sooner than necessary. The longer she was able to stay on good old *terra firma*, the better the chance that something would come up and cancel the actual flight.

After twenty minutes, Martin said, "Pull the plane off to the side of the runway, and we'll go over the flight plan. We have to wait until Jessica finishes her practice runs before we can proceed with our takeoff."

While Jessica went through the same drill that Karina had just completed, Martin patiently explained each step of the flight. "I'll take the plane up, Karina. All you need to do is keep your hands on the control stick to feel how the controls respond during takeoff. Once we clear the ground and achieve an altitude of 1000-feet above ground level, you'll take over the control stick. Just keep the wings level and climb on up to an altitude of 1800-feet. I'll work the throttle on this trip, so you don't need to worry about controlling the ultralight's airspeed."

"What should I do when we reach 1800-feet?" Karina asked, trying to hide the trembling in her voice.

"Once we arrive at 1800-feet, you'll practice flying straight and level without losing altitude, perform slow turns to the left and right, and initiate stalls," Martin continued. "That will consume most of our flight time. Then, I'll land the plane, while you follow along holding onto the control stick, just like during takeoff."

Martin finished giving instructions, leaving her a few anxious minutes for reflection. Jessica seemed to be having trouble making *Blue Bird* move in a straight line. Karina felt sick. Her mind wandered to that fateful night six years earlier, and her breathing increased until she felt light-headed. Martin had to physically grab hold of her shoulder to calm her down.

Silently, she prayed that she would get through this horrible experience. Then, as usual in stressful situations, she got angry. She'd show them. That judge had put her here just to torment her. Well, she'd show him, too.

It was almost a relief when Martin told her it was time. She brought the ultralight's nose around and pointed it down the runway. They were to be first.

Slowly, the plane began its run. Martin increased power, and the plane shot forward until its nose lifted. The ground fell away beneath them. Karina trembled uncontrollably. They were airborne!

Chapter 3

Blue Horizons

Karina closed her eyes and allowed Martin to control the ultralight, climbing steeply upward, higher and higher. Escaping the terror of the moment, she let her mind drift back to her first day at the private alternative school named Blue Horizons. Located in upstate New York at a small ultralight airfield, the school consisted of seven large curved-metal Quonset huts sectioned off into living quarters, classrooms, a mess hall and an infirmary.

Blue Horizons was small as schools go, supporting only three instructors, a staff of four, and a maximum student population of twenty. The curriculum centered on students building and flying ultralight airplanes. Learning to fly was not optional; math, science, language arts and all other subjects were incorporated into flight instruction.

Students entered the twelve-month, year-round program for two years. With luck and good behavior, students earned phone privileges in a mere three weeks. Four months without major rule infractions bought a coveted day-trip into town or home, if home was close enough. Some students at Blue Horizons came from as far away as California.

During a two-week break at the end of each year, students could be released to the custody of their parents for summer vacation, depending on whether or not all parts of the curriculum had been passed with a score of 85 percent or better. This was extremely difficult because the courses included technical reading, algebra, geometry, physics, meteorology and other difficult subjects. Most students arriving at Blue Horizons were far behind in their studies for one reason or another.

At first, Karina rebelled. Stepping defiantly from the school van that had deposited her at Blue Horizons, she told Martin, who was barking out school rules, to "lighten up" and stop acting like a dictator—which, of course, brought about immediate repercussions.

That first evening, in addition to the normal chores of cleaning up living quarters and mopping classroom floors, she had to wash dishes and clean all of the school's bathrooms, including those in the boys' living area. Karina had thought about refusing, but when Martin stood in front of her and briskly asked if she had anything else to say, her nerve failed. All she could do was shake her head. Midnight came and went before she finally got to bed. Add to that an outrageous six o'clock wake-up call, and it made for a really lousy start.

During her second week, after daily schedules had settled into routine, the first ultralights arrived. The huge kits were unloaded, and students devoted the day to inventorying parts, counting the hundreds of pieces that were destined to become flyable airplanes. What a bore! But the welded fuselage held everyone's interest—everyone, but her. She stayed as far away from the main ultralight sections as possible, wanting nothing to do with anything resembling an airplane.

That very night, she had a horrible nightmare. Angry to the core, she had hardly spoken to anyone for almost a week and might have remained completely silent, except for Jessica, her infectious roommate. Jessica had a sense of humor that could win anyone over, and in time, Karina melted.

* * *

"Okay, Karina. Take control." Martin interrupted her reverie. He had leveled the airplane, and her altimeter read exactly 1800-feet. "Don't over-control…easy movements. If you let it, this plane can almost fly itself. Maintain a heading of two—eight—zero degrees and watch your horizon. We want to maintain this altitude."

The moment she had dreaded was at hand, thrust upon her whether she was ready for it or not. Karina clutched the control stick harder than necessary. Breathing in short gasps, she yanked on the control stick with sweat-dampened hands. The plane's nose tilted sharply upward, eliminating all view of the ground. In that same panic-stricken moment, the left wing dropped, throwing the plane into a spinning dive, with the altitude dropping as if the bottom had fallen out from the sky.

"Help!" Karina screamed, control stick completely forgotten. Placing both hands against the instrument panel, she pushed against it, as if she could possibly stop their descent through sheer will power. "We're falling!"

The ultralight spun around and around, rotating toward the ground. Seated in front, Karina saw the forest-covered hills far below.

"Karina, take hold of the control stick." Martin's voice was soft, but firm. "Get the wings level, and the plane will take care of the rest."

"No! I can't!" Karina yelled, but her hands rushed forward acquiring a chokehold on the control stick. Trying to level the wings, she moved the stick to the right, and to her surprise, it worked. In fact, it worked so well that the plane's left wing came up, and the right wing went down. The plane began to spin and drop to the right.

"You're overcontrolling," Martin said. "Use only your right hand. Remove your left hand, and move the stick slowly to the left. That's it."

Almost magically, the plane stopped spinning. With gentle pressure, the wings rose, leveling the ultralight. This time, Karina was careful not to overcorrect. She was breathing hard and felt sick, but noticed that what had seemed like forever had taken only a few seconds. According to her altimeter, they had descended to about 1400-feet, not far below their planned altitude.

"What happened?" she asked, her voice shaking. "Why did it feel like we were falling?"

"That feeling of falling is what happens when the plane stalls," Martin said. "You brought the nose up too high, too fast. That caused our air speed to drop below 38-miles per hour. We didn't have enough lift to stay in flight, and we started falling. We stay in flight as long as we keep our air speed above 38-miles per hour. You have now had your first lesson on stalls, so let's try level flight, okay?"

"You have my full cooperation," Karina said. She kept the ultralight level and found that Martin was right. The plane did almost fly itself. After a few minutes, her confidence building, she began to experiment. She removed her right hand from the stick and let the plane fly itself, using just the rudder pedals to keep the plane heading on course.

"Not bad, Karina." Martin patted her shoulder. "Now let's try a slow turn to the left. Remember to keep the nose level. Keep the little ball in the center-of-gravity indicator between the two hash marks. That will keep us in a controlled turn."

"Turning left." Karina pushed gently down on the left rudder pedal and moved the control stick gently to the left. Immediately, the ultralight responded. The left wing went down about thirty degrees, and the plane began a slow left turn. Still, about halfway through the turn, something seemed wrong. Karina had that feeling she got when sitting in a car going quickly around a sharp curve. It felt as if she were sliding across her seat toward the plane's opposite side.

"Ease up on the rudder." Martin's words came through her headset. "Watch the center-of-gravity indicator. Keep the ball centered between the hash marks."

Karina did as Martin told her, and the sliding sensation vanished when the little ball in the indicator repositioned itself between the two center marks. At the same time, Karina noticed that her breathing was close to normal and the sick feeling had gone from her stomach. Maybe this flying stuff wouldn't be too bad after all.

Martin complimented her again as she pulled out of the 180-degree turn. "Not bad for a beginner. You seem to come by flying naturally. Relax a little and enjoy it. Fly straight and level on a course of 100-degrees until I tell you to turn."

Karina did as Martin directed and followed each of his instructions to the letter. They practiced 90-, 180-, and 360-degree turns. Then, with considerable urging, Martin forced Karina to pull the nose of the ultralight up until it stalled again. When Martin told her she had to deliberately stall the airplane, Karina almost forgot herself and asked if he was crazy. However, she discovered that when the wings were kept level, which of course was the goal of normal flight, all that happened was that the airplane's nose dropped sharply downward and then quickly righted itself. They were flying level again.

All was going very well, and after an hour and a half, Karina was beginning to believe that she might even like flying. Somehow, it seemed different when she was at the controls. The sensation that she was in control eased her tension.

Then, with a few simple instructions, Martin crushed her feelings of confidence like a small ship smashing against a rocky coast during a hurricane. "Karina, it's time to prepare for landing. We'll fly twice around the field, line up on the runway, and land south to north. I'll handle the landing. You lightly hold the control stick to get a feel for landing the plane."

It sounded simple enough, and everything began well, but Karina felt a sudden tightening in her chest. She circled the landing field, going through the downwind, crosswind, and upwind legs with ease. Almost perfectly, she lined up on the center of the little grass strip called Mitchum Field. Only her rapid breathing betrayed the inner turmoil that pitted her recent sense of accomplishment against nightmares from her childhood.

Martin took over and put the plane on a glide scope for landing. It was then that her world fell apart. She didn't even feel it coming, but that old pent-up fear suddenly seized control. She was watching the ground looming before them when it happened. Her hand tightened on the control stick, and she pulled up with every ounce of strength she possessed.

"Karina, what are you doing?" Martin yelled through her headset. "Let go at once!"

Fear gave her strength far beyond her 96-pounds, and she struggled against Martin for control of the ultralight. The plane's nose rose sharply. That all too-familiar feeling of falling overcame her again, and she pulled even harder on the control stick, willing the plane to stay in the air. Martin's orders to release the controls went totally unheeded.

They flew over the runway, heading straight for the trees that lined both sides of the little valley. Martin increased power but was not able to wrestle the plane's control from her. Then, what felt like a brick hit her square in the back of the head. The stick slipped from her hands as her head slammed forward, and in that instant, Martin had control. By the time she wrapped her hands back around the control stick, he had landed the plane in a small field next to the runway, about a hundred yards from where it should have been.

Once again, she pulled on the stick with all her strength. Only this time, there was no resistance from Martin. The little plane was on the ground and the control stick had no effect on the direction of the plane. Martin was in firm control of the throttle—the power necessary for movement and flight.

"Karina, stop screaming." Martin's voice rang calmly, but firmly in her ears, and she heard her own voice yelling loudly to let her out. "We're on the ground. Everything is okay. Sorry I hit you, but I had to gain control or we would have ended up in the trees."

She stopped screaming. The terror that gripped her became rage. Restrained emotion, now uncontrolled and unchecked, put Karina into the worst temper tantrum she had ever displayed. She banged her hands on the control panel and kicked the interior part of the plane's nose.

When the plane rolled to a stop and Martin raised the canopy to give her an avenue for escape, Karina fled from the airplane and headed for the woods. Her heart pumped as frantically as her legs pounded the hard, dry earth. Her lungs burned from the exertion. Karina had no idea where she was headed. Panic—not rational thought—directed her movements. Her mind was filled with the night of the crash. Under the clear blue sky, the thunder and lightning dredged from her subconscious instilled terror. She was running for her life—running to join her parents.

Chapter 4

A Day of Reckoning

Karina ran blindly, her eyes half-closed, not knowing where she was heading. Near the edge of the woods, under the towering maple trees, a gnarled tree root caught the edge of her tennis shoe.

Karina stumbled another few steps before her weary legs gave out. She crashed to the ground, then scrambled forward on hands and knees. Martin grabbed her leg and restrained any further forward progress. Sally Truman, another Blue Horizons instructor, arrived and helped Martin pin her down, holding her immobile until they could get a better hold on her. Together, Martin and Sally carried Karina kicking and screaming to her room and restrained her until the school doctor came and gave her something to calm her down.

During the period before the medication soothed Karina's anxiety, Jessica and Sally restrained her both physically and vocally with a continuous stream of soothing conversation, none of which she later remembered.

Under the medicine's influence, fear dissolved, bringing the world more into focus. With that focus, the furious pent-up emotion drained away, leaving her feeling like a limp rag doll.

Martin entered and instructed everyone, except Sally, to leave. Karina was ordered into bed and told to remain there until the doctor saw her again.

She suddenly felt ashamed, like a little girl who had just been very naughty, and the tears came. Later, she didn't remember how long she cried, but it was long enough for sleep to gain control.

Because of the emotional letdown and the medication, Karina slept through the day and all that night without so much as a dream. It wasn't until almost ten o'clock the next morning that she awoke to find herself alone in her room. She had been undressed and was in her nightshirt. For once, she was not soaking with sweat.

As events from the day before came into focus, she pulled the covers over her head and began blubbering like a little baby. Crying brought back the anger again, but not explosively this time, just defeatedly. She had made a fool of herself, and nobody was going to let her forget it. She would be the laughingstock of the entire school. And, what would Martin do to her? Whatever the punishment, she deserved it. She had almost killed them both in those final seconds before landing. For a long time, she lay under her sheets crying, until once again sleep ended her torment.

* * *

It was to a dark world and her roommate's deep rhythmic breathing that Karina awoke. Her fingers searched downward for the nightstand beside her bed, probing for her watch. It was after eleven o'clock at night. She had been in bed more than thirty hours!

Quietly, she got out of bed, slipped her feet into thongs, and pulled on a robe. After using the bathroom, Karina decided she would see if there was anything to eat in the mess hall. She was starving and snacks were often available. It was the one really nice thing about Blue Horizons: the food. There was always plenty at meals, and it was pretty good. Between meals, snacks were kept in bowls on the serving counter, usually cookies, brownies, and fruit. The instructors seemed to understand the eating needs of teens, or maybe they just liked having plenty of food around for their own purposes. Either way, she hoped something would be out. This late at night, nobody should be up. If she was quick, she could get some brownies and milk before she met anyone. Oh, it wasn't a big deal to get up and get food at night, but she was still too embarrassed to speak with anyone. She hadn't figured out how she was going to face the rest of the kids, not to mention the staff and Martin.

A soft, cool breeze met her as she opened the door and sneaked out. The air smelled clean and fresh. The night sky was clear and stars shined brightly, only to be outdone by the radiance of a magnificent full moon. She crossed the distance to the mess hall thinking about what a beautiful place this was. If only Blue Horizons hadn't selected Mitchum Field as a place of business and if the ultralights disappeared, she could really enjoy being here.

Karina inched open the mess hall door and peeked inside. A night-light always burned in case anyone needed an instructor. The instructors' rooms were located at the rear of the mess hall, which made it easy for them to help supervise meals and group meetings. Two nights a week, the entire school was treated to a movie. Because there were no televisions or radios allowed in individual rooms, these movies were a treat.

Well, she certainly wouldn't be seeing any movies for a long time. Losing free time and movie privileges were standard punishments for small rule infractions or inappropriate behavior. The demonstration she had displayed would, on a scale from one to ten—with ten being an absolute disaster—hang in there somewhere around a fifteen. For her, movies and free time were history, besides whatever other torture awaited her.

Good, the bowl was filled with chocolate brownies, and the cold milk dispenser was unlatched. Karina took three huge brownies from the bowl, helped herself to a pint milk carton, and sat down near the end of one of the long tables. She munched slowly, rehearsing in her mind scenario after scenario of what she would say to the other students when they asked her what happened. She was so deep in thought that she didn't even hear footsteps until lights flooded the mess hall, and she found herself looking straight at the last person in the world that she wanted to meet, Martin.

"Oh, Karina. It's you." Martin's voice didn't sound surprised or threatening. In fact, it seemed as if he was trying to make his voice as noncommittal as possible. His usual authoritative voice was somehow softer than normal. He walked toward her.

Karina wanted to crawl under the table. This chance meeting was not in any of her scenarios. She wanted to run, but forced herself to continue chewing on a brownie. At least with her mouth full, Martin would have to initiate any conversation.

Martin sat down onto the bench across from her. "Feeling better? You had everyone worried."

Karina gulped a mouthful of milk, washing down the brownie. "Sorry. I don't know what came over me." She felt close to tears again and shoved another huge bite of brownie into her mouth. Her eyes studied the red-and-white checkered tablecloth. She couldn't force herself to look Martin in the eyes.

"It's okay to be afraid, Karina. Everyone has fears." Martin's words surprised her. She didn't believe he was frightened of anything. "It's how you handle fear that's important. Understand?"

Slowly, she shook her head. She wanted to agree with him, so the issue would be dropped, but she couldn't force herself to lie. "I'm not sure I understand anything anymore. Everything I do is wrong. No matter how hard I work, my grades stink. My family can't stand me, and I can't stand them. I wake up in a cold sweat more nights than not, and frankly, I don't like you. Nothing personal. I'm not sure I truly like anybody, especially me."

Her final words brought tears. She shoved the last piece of brownie into her mouth, wiped her eyes with a sleeve, and stood up to leave. She had every intention of departing before she had to say more.

Martin motioned for her to sit down. "Don't go yet, Karina." Martin's voice was soft but not pleading. This was a command, not a request.

Karina thought about ignoring him but was too tired for a fight. The previous day's emotion and anger left her drained of the energy needed to challenge Martin's authority. She lowered herself to the bench. Her eyes studied leftover brownie crumbs lying in disarray on the otherwise spotless tabletop. She dabbed at tears with her sleeve.

"Fear can be a terrible thing. It can cause perfectly calm, ordinary people to engage in actions they would never consider doing under different circumstances," Martin said slowly, patiently. "What's even worse, though, is anger. Fear may have caused you to lose control as we were landing, but it was cold, hard rage that did the most damage. A rage that you are going to have to deal with, or it will destroy you."

Karina's face lifted, and her gaze met Martin's. For a long moment, they sat eye-to-eye trying to search each other out, emotions running wildly through Karina. Embarrassment—she had belittled herself in front of the other students. Shame—she had acted like a two-year-old child in an uncontrollable temper tantrum. Anger—who was this man to talk to her this way? What did he know anyway, and why shouldn't she be angry? Her world had been turned upside down six years ago, and it was never going to be righted again.

Suddenly, Martin smiled. His blue eyes sparkled behind dark-rimmed glasses and he slowly shook his head. "Hold on, young lady. Before you say anything, calm down and relax."

Karina bit her lip to keep from telling off this stranger, and she would have, except she was too fatigued to maintain her anger. In fact, she was so exhausted that the room began to spin. She placed her head down onto her arms, resting on the table.

"Look, Karina. Look at me." Martin's voice demanded obedience, and she obeyed. "One of the reasons you're here, one of the reasons each student is here, is to learn about himself or herself and what it takes to deal with personal demons. We all have them, young and old alike. I know your history. I know the courage you must summon just to look at those planes each day. I know much more about you than you can imagine."

"Then, why do you force me to fly?" she demanded. "I could work with the ground team, or on maintenance, or cleaning up, anything to stay on the ground."

"Sure, but that's not why you were sent to Blue Horizons." Martin's voice was matter-of-fact, not argumentative. "You see, Karina, I founded Blue Horizons to help kids reach outside themselves, deal with fears, and learn that life is so much more intriguing than their limited experiences let them imagine. You may not believe it right now, but there is a whole world out there waiting for you. And, it's going to come, whether you're ready for it or not."

While Martin talked, Karina's eyes never wavered from his face. Her heart wanted to respond to each sentence, but her mouth remained silent. Down inside, she had a vague feeling that Martin might be right. For a time in flight yesterday, or was it the day before, she had felt in control. The terror of flying, if only for the briefest time, had been set aside.

Martin said, "You can't bring your parents back, Karina. But you can go on with your life, as they would want. Your father loved flying. He wasn't afraid of it, no matter how it ended. And I'll bet, he'd be the first to tell you to go for it, to reach for the sky with all your heart."

"Really?" Karina responded sarcastically. "You think my father would have ever gotten into a plane if he knew his wife would die with him and leave his only child alone?"

"No, certainly not," Martin said, quelling a little of Karina's anger. "I'm not speaking about preventing his death or your mother's. Your father would never have placed either of you in any danger. But you have to look at the whole picture."

Martin didn't say more, and it was probably a good thing. He simply ended the conversation and said that she look exhausted and needed rest. He said he would clean up and for her to get some sleep.

Karina left silently, pondering Martin's lecture. She quietly climbed up to her bunk and lay in bed, staring at the moon for the longest time. Small wispy clouds inched their way across its shiny face, constantly changing shape. From the hills, an owl hooted and its mate answered. In the distance, a gaggle of geese placed the sound of laughter into the air, floating on the night breeze.

Martin's words echoed in her head. Was he right? Could she put her feelings behind her? Martin was correct about one thing. Her father had loved flying. He often spoke of how "alive" he felt each time he lifted off and "touched the heavens." He certainly wasn't afraid of flying, and she couldn't imagine him being happy doing anything else.

Her mother's voice came to her now; it seemed to be imprinted on her mind. Strange, she thought she'd forgotten that soft, resilient voice that never seemed worried about anything. If only she had some of her mother's traits, then life might be worth the effort. "Don't worry, darling. Everything will be all right in its own time." Karina repeated the words over and over again, speaking in sleep what she dared not consciously remember. The moon marched across the night sky toward the horizon, retreating from the coming dawn.

Chapter 5

▼

Above and Beyond

Karina sat nervously strapped into the front seat of *Jet Stream*, her ultralight training airplane. Six weeks had passed since her horrible first experience flying the compact little ultralight and the ensuing catastrophe that followed. Her punishment had been as great a surprise as the discovery that she actually enjoyed flying. She had fully expected Martin to restrict movie privileges and was prepared to wash about a million dishes. To her surprise, punishment had consisted of something even worse, something fiendish.

"Okay, Karina," Martin had said. "Your punishment for that uncontrolled display that endangered both of our lives will be 45-hours of flight time over the next three weeks. Three hours of logged flight time daily with Tuesdays and Sundays off."

Karina had exploded at this revelation, shouting and arguing for all she was worth. In the end, it didn't earn her even one minute's reprieve from flying. In fact, Martin added six lengthy essays in response to her outburst, plus an additional 10-hours of flight time.

Instantly, flying became part of her routine. Day after day, she and Martin preflighted *Jet Stream*, buckled up, and rose up into the heavens. Climbs, turns, stalls, setups for landing, landings, and takeoffs became her life. When she wasn't in an ultralight, Karina was maintaining one, or she was in one of the endless lectures associated with ground school and flight aerodynamics. She didn't want to admit it, but she had learned a lot, not just about flying, but also about herself.

After the second week, Karina discovered flying wasn't so bad. She was feeling at "home" in the little blue plane that she had learned to control with precision. Each morning during briefing, she answered more questions than anyone else. Excitement—not fear—built up as she checked her plane during preflight. She actually looked forward to each opportunity and could hardly wait for her next chance to soar into the sky.

Jessica had been a true friend, helping her with her studies and quizzing her each evening. They even gave up movies to cram a little more. Jessica was already soloing, and Karina had looked forward to this day—her first solo flight. Now, she would finally put herself to the test and hopefully conquer her fears. Her only concern was how isolated she felt sitting in front all alone. What if she lost control?

She would pilot from the front seat because that was where the pilot sat when flying alone in a two-seat ultralight. The center of gravity was thrown off by the weight of the engine behind the canopy when only one person was in the plane; therefore, a solo pilot flying alone sat in front to counterbalance the engine's weight. However, if she ever wanted to be an instructor and fly with a passenger, she would eventually have to learn to fly from the back seat also, not that she had any desire to become an instructor.

Though flying had taken up most of her time, there had been one terrific day that she would forever remember, the day of Joe's solo. Joe had been so nervous about the flight. He was standing beside *Blue Bird* waiting for Martin, and she was performing routine maintenance on *Jet Stream*. She walked over and started a conversation that led to a wonderful afternoon of calming Joe and reassuring him before takeoff, observing his solo experience, and then going into town for a burger and malt at the local teen hangout.

It was her first time away from Blue Horizons. Martin drove them into town—Joe, Paul, Jessica, and Karina. He told them they had until ten o'clock that evening to enjoy themselves and instructed them to stay out of trouble. Then, Martin was gone and they had the town to themselves.

First came a delightful dinner of hamburgers, fries and a delicious chocolate malt, with light excited conversation about flying in general and, specifically, Joe's solo. During that time, Joe took Karina's hand and her heart melted. Then they went to a movie in a real theater. It was a hilarious comedy, a remake of *The Parent Trap*. Joe sat beside her, his arm snugly around her shoulders. Finally, just before Martin arrived outside the theater to haul them back to Blue Horizons, came the highlight of the evening: Joe put his arms around her, pulled her close and kissed her. It was a quick, tentative kiss, but one that made her heart flutter.

* * *

"*Jet Stream*, this is control. Radio check, do you copy? Over." Martin's voice in her headset brought her back to reality. This was her day, her time to solo.

She pressed the transmit button on her radio. "Control, this is *Jet Stream*. I copy five-by-five." Five-by-five was the coded response to indicate that she heard Martin loud and clear. "*Jet Stream* preflighted and ready for northbound takeoff. Over."

The next response both thrilled and frightened Karina. "*Jet Stream*, you are cleared for takeoff. The pattern is clockwise, field altitude is 2800-feet, and wind is steady from the north at five knots. It's all yours, Karina. Be careful. Over."

Karina pushed her throttle forward and gave the ultralight the power it needed to roll slowly down the taxiway to the south end of the grass runway. Martin insisted on being formal about takeoffs and landings, as if they were landing at a regular airport. He wanted them to be prepared for any situation while flying. Maybe some day, they would have to make an emergency landing at a controlled airport.

Martin reminded her of the flight plan to which they had both agreed. "Remember, climb to pattern altitude, circle the field twice and land. Over." This would be a simple solo, nothing fancy: takeoff, circle the field, land, and repeat the process three times. Joe's solo had been much longer and more intense, but Joe had never freaked out in flight. Oh well, everyone had to start somewhere.

"Climb to pattern altitude, circle twice, and land. Over," Karina said, using the correct manner to affirm that a message had been received and understood. Moving the plane onto the south end of the runway, she took a deep breath and keyed her radio. "Taking off. Over."

She pushed the throttle fully forward. Every ounce of power the 503-cubic-centimeter, 52-horsepower Rotax engine could give her would be used on takeoff. The plane moved forward, slowly at first, then faster and faster. Karina kept one eye on the runway and the other on her airspeed indicator. She knew that her plane could leave the ground at between 38- and 40-miles per hour, but she needed the plane's speed to reach 55-miles per hour to ensure a safe transition from taxi to flight. Something called ground effect took place next to the surface. For a height equal to the ultralight's 32-foot wingspan, the turbulence caused by air flowing around her wingtips would give her increased lift. After that, if she didn't have enough airspeed to sustain flight, she would lose her lift, stall and come crashing down.

"Looking good." Martin sounded pleased. "You've come a long way, girl. Over."

The ground quickly fell away beneath her and she climbed above the trees. Higher and higher she climbed, keeping her airspeed at a steady 55-miles per hour. At 2800-feet, she began a slow clockwise turn away from the runway.

Karina thought to herself, *Now I've done it. I'm up. I've got to land this thing.* But, she was no longer frightened. Was this how her father felt the first time he'd reached for the heavens?

"How are you doing, Karina? Over." Martin asked.

"Fine," she said, leveling the plane and continuing her pattern around the ultralight field. "This is so awesome. Over."

"Don't let it go to your head. Keep your eyes on those instruments and follow your flight plan. Over," said a new voice through her headset.

Karina's heart skipped a beat. "Joe, is that you? Over." She couldn't believe her luck. Martin never let anyone else talk to a rookie during a solo.

"Yeah, but you stay focused, or Martin's going to have both our heads. Watch what you say. Big Brother is listening. Over." Joe had an easygoing manner that made him seem older than his sixteen years.

"And don't you forget it," Martin said. "Set up for landing. Over."

Karina circled the field and turned into the downwind leg of the landing pattern. She checked her position carefully. If she turned crosswind too soon, she wouldn't have enough distance to make her landing and would have to circle again. That would not please Martin, and she wanted to impress Joe.

"*Jet Stream* to control, beginning final approach. Over." She lined up on the grass runway and began her descent, cutting power back to about one-third. As power dropped, the plane floated downward toward the ground. Karina watched the little matchbox houses and stick figures grow larger. Keeping the plane's nose centered on the runway, she maintained a close watch on her airspeed. Martin had told her at least a thousand times: pitch for airspeed, power for altitude. She must position the nose of the plane just right to keep her airspeed at 55-miles per hour, her landing speed. That was how airspeed was maintained in flight, by pointing the nose of the plane at an angle that kept airspeed constant. If she wanted to climb, she increased power. To land, she decreased power. But, no matter what, she wanted to keep a steady airspeed.

"Well done. Over," Joe said upon her landing.

"Perfect," Martin said. "Now increase power and take off again. Over."

Karina was thrilled. She had done it. Twice more she took off, circled the field, and set her plane down perfectly. Martin and Joe were both impressed. She wanted to fly more, but Martin insisted they debrief and discuss the next day's flight. She would have to do some studying for it, because tomorrow Martin was going to push her to the limit.

That night, she celebrated by stuffing herself with ice cream and soda at the evening movie. Sitting as close to Joe as she dared, and with Jessica on her other side, the picture couldn't hold her attention. Her mind kept returning to the wonderful feeling of accomplishment the afternoon had given her. For the first time since the accident, Karina felt contentment. *Silly*, she thought. *How could such a small thing give her so much satisfaction?*

"Penny for your thoughts," Joe whispered into her ear. "Want some more ice cream?"

She shook her head, still smiling. "No, I'm stuffed. If I eat any more, I'll be so chubby tomorrow that Martin won't let me fly." Her voice took on Martin's mannerism, "The two-seat Challenger II ultralight is designed for a minimum 125-pound front seat weight load and can handle a front seat pilot whose maximum weight is not to exceed 250 pounds."

Joe laughed, looking Karina's slim figure up and down. "Yep, I can see it. You came in here two hours ago a lovely 98-pound slender dreamboat, and now look at you, a huge 300-pound buffalo."

"What!" Karina shouted. "Are you calling me a buffalo?"

She put her hands on Joe's chest and leaned into him, pushing him slowly backward, toward Jessica, who had assumed a hands-and-knees position behind Joe. He never even saw it coming.

"At least I'm not a klutz!" Karina giggled, extending her arms.

Joe lost his balance and ended up head-over-heels on the floor. He sprang up in a flash, chasing the two girls who had caused his fall. "Wait until I get my hands on you!"

While the rest of the group laughed at their nonsense, Karina and Jessica dodged tables and chairs, making a hasty escape toward the door with Joe in hot pursuit. Glancing over her shoulder and ducking underneath Joe's desperate lunge, Karina burst through the door and plowed right into a dark shadow intent upon entering. Karina tried to keep her balance. The figure had a death hold on her, trying to keep upright. In the end, both landed on the ground, the shadowy figure underneath and Karina above. She landed flush on top of the unidentified person's chest and heard a coarse grunt as his breath escaped from startled lips.

Things went from bad to worse as Jessica and Joe first tripped, and then sailed over the top of Karina and her prone victim. They rolled laughing and giggling into another dark shadow, but this one was able to stay upright through maneuvers similar to a football player's agility run through a series of car tires. With a hop, step, and jump at the end, came a voice each knew so well.

"What's the meaning of this nonsense?" Martin's voice expressed his outrage but also held a hint of amusement as he surveyed the damage. "If your flying is as deplorable as your earthbound modes of travel, the world is in for some really hard times ahead."

Martin reached down, grabbed hold of Karina's jumpsuit and lifted her from the startled bystander pinned underneath her and gasping for breath. "Karina, explain yourself."

She sincerely expressed her apology. "Sorry. We didn't mean any harm. We were just fooling around. It was dumb of me to run out without looking. Are you okay?" She extended a hand to the shadowy figure who turned out to be a plump little man not much taller than Martin, but considerably broader. He wore narrow, shiny-rimmed glasses that gave him a grandfatherly look.

"We didn't mean to hurt anyone," she said. "We were just playing a kind of…tag." This last comment brought giggles from Jessica and Joe, who had regained their own footing and were trying to stay as far away from Martin as possible.

"Yes, we're very sorry," Jessica said. "Did we hurt you?"

The little man rose slowly to his feet, dusted off his dark blue suit, and gathered himself together. "No serious damage done, I believe. But I must say, Martin, next time I come, you will lead."

Joe also added his regrets. Martin apologized for the unexpected onslaught, gave the kids one of his "we will speak about this later" looks, and ushered the little man inside before further damage could occur.

They followed Martin, wondering who the stranger was and why he was at Blue Horizons so late. It was nearly ten o'clock curfew time. They seldom had visitors, including parents. When they did, it was always daytime so Martin could display what they were doing and learning. Blue Horizons wasn't much on public relations. Most of the school's funding came from the tuition wealthy parents paid to straighten out a wayward teen or from state judicial systems, as in Karina's case. Neither was excited about publicity, so the arrival of this stout man near the end of the evening was very intriguing.

Upon Martin's command for quiet and attention, it became clear that the rest of the kids and instructors felt the same way. Everyone quickly gathered around Martin and his companion. All eyes scrutinized the pair, and mouths were closed.

Martin said, "I'd like to introduce a close personal friend, Mr. John Smithson. He's here to solicit our support for a project he is developing. I'll let him introduce himself further and explain the details, but I would appreciate everyone listening carefully and quietly. Let him finish before asking questions. He has already had an astonishing first impression of our program."

These last words were directed at Karina, and everyone's eyes turned toward her. She felt her face turning different shades of red and would have said something to defend herself, but Mr. Smithson interceded.

"Oh, that was nothing, just a reminder that one should always be aware of one's surroundings," Mr. Smithson said. He winked at Karina. "Actually, I'm here because I have a great deal of respect for the challenges teens face growing up today. All of you have faced some of those challenges, or you wouldn't be here. From what I've heard, you have taken on real-life learning and are putting it to the test. I am founder of the Harsten Corporation. We do research and development on curricula being employed by today's alternative or innovative schools of learning."

Mr. Smithson paused for a moment and made sure everyone was listening. "I've been observing the progress students have made after completing the program here at Blue Horizons and have been greatly impressed. But to make a terribly long, boring story short, I've been granted $500,000 to initiate a real-life adventure and then track the results such an experience imparts onto the young people who participate in the project."

At the mention of $500,000, silence, quiet enough to hear a heartbeat, overcame the group. Instructors and students, immobile as statues, waited for the little man to continue.

"My proposal is this," he said. "Find a good school with an innovative curriculum and challenge the students and staff to push their skills, talents and character to the limit. With the type of program being run here and the quality of staff on hand, I believe this is the perfect school. I am suggesting that Blue Horizons train its students for a community service flight across the United States, landing in small towns and cities along the way to encourage other youth to reach beyond themselves."

He paused again, waiting for the full effects of his words to produce the inevitable questions. "What do you think? Is Blue Horizons up to the challenge?"

"Sir?" Paul raised his hand. "You mean fly all the way to the Pacific Coast? In ultralights, that's going to be some challenge. Do you know what our airspeed and range are?"

Mr. Smithson chuckled. "Yes, I'm well aware of the capabilities of your ultralights. I've purchased four from Blue Horizons over the last three years. I told you it would be a challenge."

The others began asking question after question. What route would they take? How many planes would they use? Where would they sleep?

What about the mountains? Where would they end up, California or Washington? What about ground support?

Karina barely listened. She pictured herself flying from town to town, every day seeing new sights, every morning a new destination. Suddenly, Karina realized she wanted this opportunity, this chance to prove something to herself.

"Okay, guys, that's enough for tonight," Martin said to interrupt the endless barrage of questions. "I'll fill in the details tomorrow. What we really wanted to know tonight is whether or not you're interested in the idea."

"You bet we are," Sarah said, speaking for the group. "When do we start?"

Mr. Smithson turned to Martin, who waved off any more questions. "When we're ready and not before. Right now, however, it's time for this to end. We'll have a full briefing in the morning. Everyone head for bed."

"What do you think?" Karina asked Jessica. "Do I have a chance of being picked as one of the pilots?" She had been worried about that. Her track record was probably the shakiest of anyone currently at Blue Horizons. Why would Martin choose her to fly? She knew that only five or six of the kids would be chosen, and only Valerie had spoken out against piloting one of the ultralights. That left thirteen other kids besides herself. Jessica and Joe were sure to get the chance. They were the two top-rated pilots of the class. She had so many strikes against her—her early fear and tantrums, her grades, her ability to break rules, even charging into the man who was making all of this possible.

"You really want to be a pilot?" Jessica's voice held a hint of surprise. "This is going to be the greatest challenge Blue Horizons has ever attempted. Soft field landings, mountain updrafts to contend with, desert thermals. Are you sure you can do it?"

Karina shifted her position to get a better view of Jessica's bed. Jessica was lying on one side, facing Karina, and the two girls locked eyes in the dimness provided by the tiny night-light on Jessica's desk. She said thoughtfully, "Other than getting my parents back, I have never wanted anything more. If I can do this, maybe things will be better for me later. I don't know how to explain it, but I desperately need this chance."

For a long moment, neither girl spoke. Then, Jessica climbed down and went to Karina's bed. She climbed up next to Karina and took her hands. "Then, let's make it happen."

Karina hugged Jessica and the two plotted late into the night. Their battle strategy was simple. Karina was going to become the smartest, best-qualified pilot Blue Horizons had ever seen, and Jessica was going to help her.

The days that followed were so filled with activity that the Blue Horizons kids hardly had time to breath. Evening movies gave way to additional lectures and films on emergency landing procedures, formation flying, and weather patterns. Airplane maintenance, flying and final construction of the last single-seat ultralight consumed every daytime minute.

Every student, except Valerie, was vying for one of the coveted pilot positions. Only five students would pilot planes cross-country. Each would fly one of the four single-seat airplanes using a rotation schedule. Each pilot would fly four days and rest one. The flight course was over 5000-miles long and encompassed 19 states. Competition became intense, but Karina was still in the running. She had been mildly surprised and thankful that Martin had not denied her the chance. She had half expected him to laugh at her when she told him that next morning she wanted to be a pilot. Martin had only asked if she fully understood what she was letting herself in for.

"Formation flying requires great concentration and a lot of practice," Martin had said. "And another thing, when you fly alone, the only person at risk is you. When you fly with a team, every pilot has a responsibility to the rest of the pilots in the formation. Are you ready for that kind of responsibility?"

Karina had thoughtfully said, "Yes, I think so." And from that moment on, she worked diligently. When she wasn't flying, she was hitting the books with Jessica and Joe. Joe had taken her under his wing too, which was good for Karina. Not only did she have the pleasure of being with the boy she liked, but he was also the most knowledgeable pilot in the group. Only instructors, Martin and Sally, knew more about flying.

Because of her previous "punishment" hours, Karina had more flight hours than most other students at Blue Horizons. She made the adjustment to the small single-seat airplanes with ease. They were actually easier to fly than the two-seat ultralights. With a lower stall speed, the single-seat Challengers could land and takeoff on a football field-sized area. They were also equipped with the added security of an emergency parachute fastened to the top of the plane's canopy. The parachute was rocket propelled and could be used in the event of a catastrophic emergency, such as losing a wing in flight. At all other times, the pilot should be able to set down. A 20-to-1 glide ratio gave the pilot 20 or more miles to find a suitable landing spot, and on a day with good wind conditions, those little planes had been known to stay aloft for over an hour without engine power, gliding on wind currents.

Karina excelled on landings. Among the students, only Joe and Jessica were her equal. But, she still had to prove that she could handle stress and emergency situations. She had overheard Martin telling Sally that he wasn't sure she was ready for the challenge that this cross-country flight had in store for them. At least he seemed willing to give her the chance. He hadn't pulled her from the competition. For that, she was truly grateful.

A week later, they were roused out of bed earlier than usual, five o'clock. Everyone had been told to gather flight gear and report to the ready room after a quick breakfast of scrambled eggs and cereal.

"Have a seat, people," Martin said as they filed into Classroom 3 for briefing. "Today, we're going to see how you handle soft field emergency landings on a short field surrounded by vertical obstructions."

Karina seated herself next to Jessica and flipped open her notebook. "Wish me luck." Jessica smiled her return.

"Megan?" Martin asked. "What's the most important thing to remember about soft field landings?"

"Keep the nose wheel up for as long as possible in order to let the main wheels touch down first," Megan said.

"Good." Martin was pleased. "Karina, why is it important for the main wheels to touch down first?"

Karina responded without hesitation. "Because if the nose wheel touches down onto soft earth before the main wheels, the nose wheel may dig into the ground, allowing momentum to lift the tail and flip the plane over onto its back."

"Excellent," Martin said after grilling each student. "You all understand the theory. Now, let's see how you handle the practical. We'll take off and fly on a heading of zero—three—zero degrees for about five miles. There you will find a small deserted field that we have permission to use for this little exercise. This field lies in the middle of a small valley surrounded by trees. Now, to keep this test safe, we have set out marker flags to indicate the vertical altitude that must be maintained on your approach. Sally or I will fly down beside you while you land to determine if you have maintained a safe altitude. Remember, there are real trees at the end of this field, so don't lose track of your position."

Karina made notes on her kneeboard about the trees, correct altitude and other details Martin provided. She was nervous. So much was riding on her performance during this exercise. Martin would be noting every single move she made. Even the tone of her voice was important. She couldn't sound anxious or stressed. It would take only one small mistake to exclude her from further consideration. Today, she had to be perfect.

Martin said, "Plane assignments are as follows: Paul is in *Humming Bird*. Devon is in *Sparrow*. Katie's got *Lady Bird*, and Karina's flying *Meadow Lark*. Afternoon assignments will be announced at the one o'clock briefing. Sally will fly support for Paul and Katie. I'll support Devon and Karina. Maintenance teams have one hour to prepare all planes. Pilots begin preflight in 90 minutes. Ground support leaves immediately. Any questions?"

There were no other questions, and everyone, except the pilots, headed for the exit. When the room cleared, Martin and Sally went over weather conditions with the pilots. Martin explained that they were leaving so early because the wind had been still most of the night, and the cool air would give them good lift conditions. He reminded everyone that he would be watching them closely, and warned that if Sally or he ordered an abort, they were to immediately climb to pattern altitude and circle for another attempt. He would not hold an aborted landing against them, but he would revoke their flight status immediately if they pushed the safety envelope so much as an inch. Everyone believed him, and no one said a word or made jokes to relieve the tension as they normally did before a flight that included a new procedure.

Jessica met Karina as she left the briefing room. "*Meadow Lark*'s all ready. I'm your maintenance person for today." She put her arm around Karina's shoulder.

"Thanks." Karina gave her friend a hug. Jessica's petite stature allowed Karina to stand toe-to-toe with her, and the two friends embraced tightly. The apple scent from Jessica's freshly shampooed hair somehow relaxed Karina. "I wish you were going to be with me, but I guess you've already got a pilot's spot nailed down."

"I'm not so sure about that. I wish I could be with you, or at least with the ground team. It's going to be tense waiting for you guys to get back. We'll try to listen in on the radio, but my guess is that with so much regular air traffic in this area, Martin will have you using short range radio."

They reached *Meadow Lark*, and Jessica helped Karina preflight the little single-seat ultralight. They checked each rivet, bolt, and moveable part to make sure everything was secure and working properly. Then, they checked the engine and fuel tank. The smaller plane only had a 5-gallon gas tank compared with the 10-gallon tank on the larger two-seat planes. This, combined with a smaller engine and slower airspeed, kept the little plane in compliance with Federal Aviation Administration, FAA, regulations.

Karina gave Jessica a final hug, wished each of her fellow pilots luck, fastened the buckle on her helmet, and climbed into the cramped confines of her ultralight. She was to be the last student to take off, followed only by Martin.

Jessica helped Karina fasten her shoulder harness. "Go get 'em, Tiger."

Karina gave her friend a timid smile and lowered her canopy window. She checked her radio, yelled the required "clear" before starting her engine, and taxied out to her takeoff position.

The flight to the practice field proved uneventful and would have been boring, if it weren't for what lie ahead. Karina enjoyed the view. Being last in line was a benefit. She noted on her kneeboard when Martin ordered Devon to abort and go around again. She saw where he began his turn and picked a landmark farther downwind to begin her own turn.

One after the other, Karina watched little planes set down onto the small field. Katie also had a problem. She came in too high over the simulated vertical obstacles and overshot the runway by almost 50-yards. Then, it was Karina's turn.

"*Jet Stream* to *Meadow Lark,* begin your landing run. Over," Martin said after Katie was safely down and had taxied out of the way.

"Roger, landing. Over," Karina said.

She was already at the end of the downwind leg. She slowly cut back on her throttle as she made her turn to line up for landing. She was at the correct altitude and saw Martin's plane off to her left.

Once she cleared the trees at the east end of the field, Karina concentrated on the cones that simulated tall obstacles and, thus, shortened the field to just under 80-yards. She cut back on power and increased her angle of descent, keeping her airspeed steady at 55-miles per hour. Karina picked a spot on the ground to aim for, where she wanted the main wheels to touch down.

After clearing the artificial obstacles, she pulled up sharply on the control stick. The little plane responded immediately to her adjustments. The plane leveled and her airspeed dropped sharply. Then, as the plane flew only a few feet above the ground, Karina brought the nose up farther into a flared stall, and the plane's main wheels found the ground. Shortly after, her nose wheel came down, and within a few feet, the ultralight came to a halt.

Karina didn't wait to congratulate herself. She pushed the throttle slightly forward giving the plane just enough power to taxi out of the way, so Martin could begin his landing.

"Nicely done, team," Martin said after he landed and gathered them around. "Paul, your landing was right on target. Devon, give yourself a little more downwind run. You've got enough altitude. Katie, watch your angle of descent and remember you're in ground effect. Perfect, Karina. Now, let's pull those cones in a little closer and try it again."

Perfect, Karina. Martin had said only two words, but they were music to her ears. She was so excited, she almost forgot her helmet as she climbed back into *Meadow Lark*.

"You might want this," Sally said. The tall, usually reserved, instructor handed Karina the helmet and patted her shoulder. "Nice landing."

All morning, they performed takeoffs and landings on the little farm field. With each new attempt, the cones were moved in closer and closer until they were landing in a space no longer than sixty yards. Karina was beginning to believe she could land the little plane in her aunt's backyard. Wouldn't that be something? She could imagine the shock and surprise on her aunt's face.

Upon landing back at Mitchum Field, Karina gave Jessica a thumbs-up, indicating everything went well. Her friend had been so worried about how Karina was doing that she'd bitten her fingernails down to the quick.

Nine days and countless emergency procedures later, Martin gathered them together in the mess hall during what had become evening lecture classes. Only this time, there were no quizzes, complicated weather systems, or performance diagrams posted on the blackboard. Instead, Mr. Smithson was back, this time wearing less formal clothing.

Martin motioned for the group to sit. The tension was thick enough to cut with a knife, especially for Karina. She so badly wanted to be a pilot.

No one asked when a final decision would be made about the flight for fear it would be canceled. Karina knew that Mr. Smithson was looking at two other projects as well: one in which students did scientific research in the Amazon rain forest and one that put students on ships to do marine research and reef studies.

She wrenched her sweating hands as she sat in her chair and tensely waited for the results, results that held her fate, her self-confidence, and, quite possibly, her future.

"Mr. Smithson has some information that we have all been waiting to hear," Martin said. He motioned for Mr. Smithson to take over.

"Yes, I certainly do," Mr. Smithson said. "You will be happy to hear that we have chosen the cross-country flight as our research project. All of the schools involved have done well, but I believe Blue Horizons has the greatest potential for reaching out to the community."

Karina barely heard the rest. She daydreamed about landing beside a large high school. Everyone's eyes were on her, and she was coming in for a perfect landing. Just then, a strong crosswind shoved her off course. Her left wing clipped a fence post, and the little plane flipped upside down. It slid through the fence and plowed into a parked car, which immediately burst into flames.

"Karina?" Joe's hand on her shoulder brought Karina back to reality. "You're as white as a ghost."

She looked around quickly to see if anyone noticed her rapid breathing and sweaty brow. Her heart raced. What was wrong with her? Wasn't this what she had worked so hard to hear?

"I'm fine," she said, hoping Joe wouldn't see through her lie. "I'm just excited and want so badly to be one of the pilots." She turned her attention away from Joe.

Martin now spoke to the group. "Everyone has worked so hard that choosing five pilots has been extremely difficult, and I want to remind all of you that we are a team. Every position is important."

Karina crossed her fingers, but after her daydream, she wasn't so sure being chosen would be a good thing. She bit her lip as Martin walked to the board and made three lists, one for pilots, one for maintenance, and one for weather. Everyone would have to work with public relations.

"Now, the moment for which you have waited so long." Martin wrote as he spoke. "Valerie, Devon, Jeff, Sarah and Kelly will be our maintenance crew. It will be their job to keep the planes in perfect flying order. Daily maintenance will be required."

Martin wrote the names in the maintenance column on the board as he spoke. He moved to the weather team column. Karina would soon find out by default whether or not she was going to be a pilot. The kids were all sitting on the edge of their seats.

"Katie, Sam, Carl, Jenny and Jesse will handle weather and reporting," said Martin. "That will require setting up the wind socks and weather instruments, maintaining radio control of landings and takeoffs, walking the landing fields to find any obstructions or bad spots, and updating our Internet site each day."

She was a pilot! Karina didn't know whether to laugh or cry. Joe slapped her on the back, and Jessica jumped up and down. Paul and Megan congratulated each other.

"Settle down. Let me finish," Martin said. "That, of course, leaves Joe, Jessica, Paul, Megan and Karina as our pilot team. It will be their responsibility to finish two 100-hundred-mile legs of the journey each day, weather permitting."

Martin went on to explain the entire trip would take about eight weeks. The ground team would travel in the school's two 15-passenger vans. Each van would pull a large U-Haul trailer loaded with their clothes, equipment, spare parts and personal items. Harold, the only counselor who didn't fly, would drive one of the vans and be in charge of the maintenance team. Mr. Smithson would drive the other van and take charge of the weather team.

The flight team would consist of two sections. The first, under Sally's command, included Megan, Joe and Jessica. Martin would command the second, consisting of Paul and Karina. Martin would also take responsibility for the entire flight group while it was in the air.

After all responsibilities were handed out, Martin had the kitchen staff serve ice cream, cake and soft drinks. They had the evening off, and a fresh batch of new movie releases sat on top of the VCR. Full details would be explained the following morning. The evening air was soon filled with the sounds of laughter, good-natured kidding and excited talk about the trip.

Karina's emotions wouldn't allow her to sit still for a movie, so she drifted outside with Jessica. She hoped Joe would come too but he was involved in a serious discussion with Mr. Smithson about the route they would take and what cities they would visit.

"Look at that moon." Jessica sighed, leaning against the light post. "Sometimes, I think I could fly right up and touch it."

She looked at Karina, who sat on the hood of Martin's little station wagon. "I'm so happy I could burst. What about you Karina? You're awfully quiet."

Karina said, "I'm happy, excited, worried and frightened right down to my toes."

"Frightened? Why?" Jessica unwrapped her arms from the pole and climbed up beside Karina. "You've been flying great, and you haven't had a nightmare for days."

"No, now I'm getting them in the daytime." Karina explained about her daydream and how she had crashed and burned. "Do you think my dreams have a meaning? Maybe they're premonitions about the future."

"I think you've come a long way since arriving here." Jessica chose her words carefully. "When you first arrived, you really frightened me. I was afraid that you might hurt yourself or me."

Jessica took Karina's hands in hers. "Now, I think I have the kindest, most devoted friend I've ever known. And, no, I don't believe your dreams are a sign of what's in the future. I think they are a link to your past, a past you're having a hard time putting behind you. But one day, you will. Perhaps this trip will be the break you need. Either way, we're going to be doing this together."

Karina hugged Jessica and the two continued talking late into the night. Martin stopped by after the others had headed for bed and told them they could stay up as late as they wanted, so long as they didn't leave the area. They could sleep longer tomorrow morning. Breakfast would be self-serve and the briefing wasn't scheduled until eleven o'clock.

Sitting together on the little porch swing outside of the mess hall, Karina and Jessica talked about childhood memories, hopes, fears, dreams, and, of course, boys. It wasn't until the moon drifted behind the hills, and the night wind chilled them, that the two girls headed for the comfort of their room.

At that moment, Karina was at peace. She felt she had gained a sister in Jessica. The evening had been like an enchanted dream, and tomorrow it would continue. She was going to be a pilot.

Chapter 6

▼

Departure

Karina completed her transition from climbing to level flight. She had begun the journey in *Meadow Lark*, her favorite ultralight. They had taken off just after dawn to avoid further publicity. Once the local newspaper in Wells, New York, discovered plans for the flight across the United States, Blue Horizons had become a media circus. Newspaper reporters and TV crews poured in from all over the state. The controversial journey made local, regional, national, and world news. Most reports had been positive, but some focused on the dangers of flying and criticized the project.

One newspaper ran a whole series of articles about programs involving students who had died during challenging ventures from school programs that the newspaper portrayed as extreme. The funny thing about that newspaper was they never even sent a reporter to Blue Horizons to get the facts straight. The kids had practically been portrayed as juvenile delinquents and the instructors as criminals for allowing students to fly airplanes. Of course, they hadn't done any research on flying either, or they would have learned that many kids learned to fly airplanes between the ages of fourteen and seventeen, which was the legal age for earning a full pilot's license.

A week before departure, publicity got so bad that concentrating on important flight readiness tasks became nearly impossible. Finally, Martin put an end to media distractions by emphasizing the importance of allowing the students to finish their lessons and preparations. Oh yes, lessons remained a part of each student's everyday experience.

Algebra was Karina's downfall. No matter how much effort she put into it, a B- was her limit. Because keeping all grades at the level of B- or above was required to maintain one's flight status, she spent many long, precious free-time hours locked away in her room being tutored by Jessica, the Blue Horizons resident math whiz.

At last, the preparations and training ended. On the evening of June 6, Martin gathered everyone together immediately after dinner and herded them over to Classroom 3 for the news. The epic journey would begin on Saturday morning, just two days away. Packing was set for Thursday, leaving Friday to spend in town relaxing and taking care of any personal business, as long as the students stayed away from the press.

The route had been finalized. The trip would take between eight and ten weeks depending on weather. They would fly between 200- and 300-miles each day, covering almost 5000-miles on a zigzag course that would take them through 12 states, less than originally planned, but enough. They would take off from Mitchum Field, just outside of Wells, New York, head west and fly around the southern borders of the Great Lakes. The journey's first leg would take them through New York, Pennsylvania, Ohio, and Indiana, finally ending up at the great airplane town of Oshkosh, Wisconsin.

While in Wisconsin, Martin promised them a surprise. What it was, he wouldn't say, and all of their begging and pestering didn't earn them even a clue. After the "surprise," they would head south through Illinois, across the Mississippi River to Missouri, then southwest to Oklahoma and into upper Texas. There, at the end of leg two, they would take a few days off to make public appearances at several alternative schools around the area.

The third leg would lead them through New Mexico, where they would head south to avoid flying over the Rocky Mountains. Even with flying south, almost to the Mexican border, they would have to fly through mountain valleys at an above sea level altitude of over 8000-feet. Mountain updrafts could become a major problem, as well as desert temperatures reaching well over 100-degrees Fahrenheit. The final stretch would cross the southern parts of Arizona and California. On that final leg out of Yuma, Arizona, they would fly across the Salton Sea, over more mountains and then land on a white sand beach next to the Pacific Ocean, just outside of the city of Oceanside, California.

Martin had promised them plenty of time on the beach, a trip to Disney Land and possibly a climb up Mount Whitney, the highest mountain in the continental United States, before they began the trip home via Amtrak. They had all protested the idea of returning by train, but Martin had explained that by the time they reached California, he would have had enough sitting in the uncomfortable cockpit of an ultralight airplane, and he suspected they would have similar feelings. They had assured him they wouldn't, but Martin had just smiled and said, "wait and see."

* * *

"*Jet Stream* to *Meadow Lark*," Martin said over the headset. "How's it going, Karina? I haven't heard a peep out of you since takeoff. Do you copy? Over."

"*Meadow Lark* to *Jet Stream*, I copy. Everything is just fine. I'm just enjoying the view. Over," Karina said. They had flown above a valley between two mountains and were now over wooded hillsides.

"How is your fuel? Over," asked Martin.

"I've got a little less than half a tank. Over," Karina said. She checked her watch and was surprised. They had been flying almost an hour and a half.

She listened as Martin checked on the others. Sally and Paul were flying just ahead of her, maybe half a mile. Joe was to her right with Jessica on his right, and Martin was a quarter mile behind, bringing up the rear. Martin also flew a hundred feet above the group, so he had a better view of the formation.

Flying in formation was tricky. Karina had to be aware of her surroundings and fellow pilots at all times. They were flying at 1800-feet above ground level, and she saw part of the ground support team on the road just ahead of them. While in the air, the formation cruised at 70-miles per hour, heading in a straight line. The ground team traveled at about the same speed and had to navigate all of the curves that the winding highway had in store for them.

At first, Karina worried that they would outdistance their support team, leaving them far behind. However, she didn't take the force of a west-to-east headwind into consideration. They were flying into a headwind of 17-miles per hour, thus her actual ground speed was only 53-miles per hour. As a result, the formation was just barely keeping up with their ground support vans.

Part of the ground team had gone ahead to prepare for their first landing and the publicity waiting for them. Karina sure hoped everything went well with landing, and the press was kind to them. She, for one, was a little tired of being under a microscope. Always remembering to be on her best behavior and watching what she said, something she wasn't very good at anyway, made her uncomfortable. Besides, she had to make a presentation to a Boys and Girls Club group at an early dinner being prepared in their honor.

Karina shifted her weight slightly. The seat was becoming uncomfortable. Martin was probably correct. By the time they had been at this for 10 weeks, another form of transportation would be most desirable. Maybe shipping the planes back to New York wasn't such a bad idea after all.

"Onward, Christian soldiers."

Her headset came alive with the familiar song. Joe was singing along with the tape. He had gotten into singing during training, and everyone was quickly becoming an expert on Christian music. Joe's singing and the music continued.

Karina keyed her microphone. "Hey, what's happening? Over."

"Just thought I'd give you heathens some inspiration," Joe said. "Just look at this beautiful sky, not a cloud in sight. And look at that lake. I've never seen such a beautiful sight in my life. Over."

"Oh, really," Jessica said sarcastically. "How is this beautiful sight so much better than the last beautiful sight we had fifteen minutes ago? Must you sing? Over."

"You trying to tell me you don't like classical Christian music? Over." Joe feigned being hurt by Jessica's remark.

"It's not your music that bothers us. It's your voice. Over," Karina said.

Secretly, everyone had to admit they actually liked Joe's singing, but letting him know wasn't "cool." Besides, he had volunteered to be the main spokesperson for all church group presentations.

"Oh, that hurts! Over." Joe said. He turned the music up and sang louder.

"Joe, Joe!" Karina yelled into her microphone. "I'll buy you an ice cream this evening if you'll only stop that caterwauling. Over."

"I'll chip in. Over," said Sally over the air.

"Me, too," others said to add their pleas.

"Triple scoop? Over." The music lowered.

"You're on. Over." Karina laughed.

Martin cut any further tirade short. "I hate to break into this amusing little conversation, but it's time to begin our approach to Williamstown. Do it just like we rehearsed. Sally leads, followed by Paul, Jessica, Joe, and Karina. I'll fly observation until everyone is down, and then join you.

Anyone who's short on fuel or needs to change formation for any other reason should shout it out now. Over."

No one had any pressing needs that required a change in rotation. The lead ground team had already arrived, checked out the area being used for a landing field, set up the windsock and was awaiting their arrival.

Martin handled the initial radio communication and discovered a ton of press waiting below. He signaled to begin landing. One after another, each pilot circled the field, checked the windsock and asked final permission from the ground team. Landing was a breeze. The pasture was huge, providing almost 600-feet in which to land.

Karina could have landed in less than a fourth that distance. But, just the same, she was happy for an easy first landing. With all the press and pressure, she didn't want any mistakes. Her approach was perfect. Cones were set up to outline an improvised runway, and crowds of people had gathered on both sides of the field.

She was on a perfect glide slope and cut her engines at just the right time. Flaring the plane's nose up, it settled smoothly onto the improvised grass runway. She taxied to the end and guided her plane to the side, lining it up next to Joe's. Several police officers were maintaining crowd control.

Karina raised *Meadow Lark*'s canopy window and removed her helmet. Removing the helmet felt wonderful. She ran her hands through her hair, hoping it wasn't a big mess. Helmets weren't exactly sensitive to the needs of a girl's hair. She climbed out and was ushered over to the group. Martin was already rolling down the runway.

The entire flight team was ushered to a wooden reviewing stand erected so everyone could see them above the crowd. Paul and Jessica did most of the talking during this initial press conference, followed by Sally and Martin. Then, they signed autographs for the little kids and a few "not so little kids" before breaking away for a much deserved bathroom break. After all, ultralights didn't provide in-flight movies or bathrooms.

They had a wonderful meal at a local Lutheran church, and Karina spent an hour speaking to kids about flying. She answered questions about living at Blue Horizons and if she would do this again if she had the chance, as well as countless other questions. At first, she was shy and had trouble getting a conversation going, but as the kids asked more questions about flying, Karina found she really enjoyed telling them about the experience. In her heart, she also hoped these kids would have the same opportunity.

About two o'clock in the afternoon, after an endless series of good-byes, they were off again. Everyone was ready to get back into the air. The crowd and excitement were great, but tiring. The ground team had it even worse. They had to wait until the planes were up before they could even begin an exit.

The maintenance team did a wonderful job of showing the press how the planes were maintained. Step-by-step, they carefully instructed the press about every aspect of airplane maintenance. Reporters noted every act while the planes were refueled and wiped down, windshields cleaned, and every moving part checked over. Blue Horizons and its students got great reviews on the news that night.

Karina piloted *Meadow Lark* down the improvised runway and up into a cloudless early summer sky. They headed west toward their last destination for the day, a little town named Walworth.

Everyone flew in silence that afternoon. Karina wasn't the only one in the group touched by the warmth and fellowship derived from the morning's layover. Each member of the group, students and adults alike, including Mr. Smithson, dwelled on the glowing attention and encouragement heaped upon them by newfound friends and kinder-than-expected news reporters.

Landing to another cheering crowd, they endured a repeat performance. Speeches, dinner, photo opportunities and autographs took up the lazy summer afternoon and early evening. Karina's interview and speech before the Girls and Boys Club was delightful. Along with Megan, who was looking for excitement after spending all day riding in a support van, the girls held their young audience enthralled with the excitement of the adventure.

That night, after all the commotion was over, the kids were parceled out among local families, two students to a family. The weary travelers welcomed a chance for relaxation and showers. A quiet night's rest was needed. This day was not an end unto itself, but the beginning of a legacy, reaching into every life it touched. With dawn would come another adventure.

Karina and Megan stayed with a friendly family, the Keegans, who owned a farm located a few miles from town. The family's six children, two boys and four girls ages three to fourteen, were a blast. Playing games of tag, hide-and-seek and Monopoly eased the day's tension and excitement.

The ten o'clock evening news devoted almost five minutes of coverage to the cross-country flight and Blue Horizons. This notoriety brought another round of explanations about the trip and all of its preparations. The girls would have been willing to stay up all night reminiscing, if it were not for Mrs. Keegan's motherly wisdom that shooed first her own children off to bed and then directed Karina and Megan toward a second floor bedroom.

The two friends shared a queen-sized bed. They were tired, but not sleepy. After changing into nightshirts, the girls sat on the bed and took turns brushing each other's hair. A soft breeze blew through the tall screened windows, filling the room with the sweet smell of apple blossoms in early June.

"What was it like up there today?" asked Megan. "I was so bored riding in the van. Everyone had something to do, but me. I can't wait to get into the air tomorrow."

Karina nodded. "Me, too. I'm glad my ground rotation day isn't until Monday. It's great up there, flying along in formation, feeling part of something wonderful. You'll love it. Coming in for a landing, the cheering crowds, the people waving and all the questions really make you feel important."

Karina finished braiding Megan's hair and placed her brush on the little table next to the bed. Megan, at nearly fifteen, was an imp, barely five feet tall and 90-pounds soaking wet. When flying in one of the two-seat ultralights, Martin had to put 65-pounds of sand bags under her seat to balance out the center of gravity and get the plane's nose wheel down to the ground.

"It's been a long time since anyone cared about what I have to say." Megan slipped back the crisp white sheets, slid underneath, and pulled them up to her chest. "I hope tomorrow is a good day for flying. I heard the weather is due to change before long."

"You'll make it up tomorrow," Karina said, sliding under the sheets next to Megan and wrapping them around her feet. "What do you mean no one cares about what you have to say?"

"Oh, it's just that my mother and father are so busy with their own lives and careers that they don't care much about what I have to say. Unlike most kids at Blue Horizons," Megan said to Karina, "I'm here because I wanted to do something my parents couldn't do. That way, maybe, they'll have some time to listen to me. If I do something to make them proud, maybe I'll be somebody to them other than 'the kid.'"

Karina reached over and turned out the lamp. "I bet your parents care more about you than you think, and if not, I'm sure they will by the time we reach California."

"I sure hope so." Megan yawned and rolled over onto her side. "Good night."

Karina pondered Megan's words and made herself a promise to become better acquainted with her tiny companion. During the time Karina had been at Blue Horizons, they had seldom spoken. Karina had been so wrapped up in her own problems that she had never even considered that others at Blue Horizons were suffering from the same insecurities. Sleep overtook her before she could sort things out.

* * *

The excitement of those first days bonded Karina to the other Blue Horizon students in a way she never could have imagined, close and caring in every word and action, up early every morning, breakfast, good byes, and briefings followed by the early morning flight. The routine continued with lunch served at their first stop, interviews, and sometimes speeches before the afternoon flight. Every evening found Karina together again with her classmates, sometimes to be parceled out among host families for the night, and sometimes for a sleepover in a local church or community center.

Ten days of good weather brought them around the southern edge of the Great Lakes and up Lake Michigan's west coast into Wisconsin. The group landed at the Oshkosh airfield. Oshkosh was well known for its annual gathering of experimental and light aircraft. They were too late for the gathering, but the community showed them plenty of hospitality. The students stayed together, dormitory-style, in a modern aircraft hangar.

"Good evening, ladies and gentlemen," Martin said, after calling for a special meeting. "I've got some interesting news for you. Have a seat."

The group grabbed folding chairs and gathered around Martin. Karina was certain that the meeting was important. Since the journey's second day, they had always had evenings to themselves.

"I promised you a few surprises on this trip," Martin said. "Here is the first. We are going to take part in a training mission for the Civil Air Patrol, otherwise known as the C.A.P. We'll simulate an overdue and downed plane situation for the C.A.P. to mount a rescue."

"How many of us get to participate?" asked Jessica. "Will we just act out a crash landing, or may we join in the search?"

"We'll send two pilots out in *Blue Bird*. They will locate a field somewhere within a few miles of their scheduled flight plan and set down near the field's edge. Then, they'll roll the plane under the cover of trees until only a small part of the tail section is visible from above," Martin said. "Sally will fly *Jet Stream* in support until the plane is safely down and ready for the exercise to begin. Then, she'll return. Sally will be the only person who knows where our pilots are located."

As Martin continued, Karina and Jessica exchanged quick glances. "When our crew is overdue at its scheduled destination, a missing plane report will be filed with the C.A.P. Captain Dave Marris, Civil Air Patrol commander for this area, will then initiate a search and rescue operation. He will be the only person among the C.A.P. participants who knows this exercise is not a real situation."

Martin said, "In answer to your last question, we will participate in the actual search operation only if requested to do so by the C.A.P. That should happen only if they have a great deal of trouble finding our downed team. Our silence about this simulation is absolutely essential to maintain the urgency of the exercise, so only those of you who can keep a lid on the loose chatter and act the part will have any chance of participating."

"Who will be the downed pilots?" Karina asked, crossing her fingers.

Martin eyed each of his pilots, a smile creeping from under his bushy mustache. "We're going to have a fly-off activity to select our pilots."

"What kind of fly-off?" Megan asked.

"Sally?" Martin gestured for her to explain.

Sally moved to the white dry erase board that traveled with them for use during lectures and classes. She quickly traced a runway with a stop sign near one end. At the other end, she drew an arrow indicating the direction of travel.

"We'll test each pilot's ability to perform a short field landing by pairing one of our pilots with a ground crew member in a two-seat ultralight. They'll take off, circle the field, and then try to land as close to the center of the stop marker as possible. The two pilots with the closest landings will be our crash landing team," Sally said. "However, there are some special circumstances that must be taken into consideration."

"Special considerations?" Joe asked.

"Yes, because our crash team may have to stay overnight, or even a couple of nights alone together, both pilots must be the same sex."

That brought a couple of snickers and nervous laughter from the group. After a few jokes, Martin interceded. "Okay, let her finish. This is important."

"Scoring will be done in this manner," Sally said. "If either Joe or Paul comes in first, they will be our pilots. If Jessica, Megan, or Karina come in first, the second-closest landing by one of the ladies will determine the second pilot, even if one of the boys has a better second place finish."

"Why are we using a ground team member for practice and not for the real thing?" Katie asked the question pointedly. "Are we only good enough for ballast, but not for real flight?"

Sally looked to Martin for an answer. An uneasy silence filled the room. This was the first comment since their journey had begun that held even a hint of dissension.

"That's a valid question, Katie," Martin answered. "However, I'm not sure I like the tone. But, I'll answer it anyway. The reason we are using ground members for the landing competition is to force each pilot to work alone and not put pressure on a specific team of pilots. With the odd number of girls in our flight team, we would have to let one girl make two attempts."

Martin moved to Katie and placed a hand on the seated girl's shoulder. "As far as your second question goes, it's not about whether or not the ground team is valuable to us or not. Each of you is very valuable. I want to maintain my flight team for this journey. The more flight experience gained, the better they will perform when we head west and run into more difficult flying conditions."

Joe slipped his hand into Karina's while Martin directed his attention toward Katie and the other ground team students. Karina knew that all the pilots were uncomfortable with Katie's challenge. She also understood that the answer to this question would determine whether the Blue

Horizons students continued to be a homogeneous group or began polarizing into competitive "cliques."

Karina's heart jumped with Joe's gesture. She squeezed his hand, getting reassurance from his firm grip. She prayed that Martin's answer to Katie's challenge would pull them together again. She had begun to think of Blue Horizons as home, and its students and staff as family. Now, she felt as if there was a family rift in progress. She held her breath, gripped Joe's hand, and anxiously waited for Martin's response.

"However, you may have a point," Martin said. "It's been more than two weeks since some of you have flown."

Martin paced back and forth, while the group breathlessly waited for him to continue. He motioned for Sally, Harold, and Mr. Smithson to join him. They huddled together near the front of the room. During this time, no one dared to speak. All eyes nervously focused on the instructors who had become so important to them. The huddle broke and Martin returned to face the group.

"How about this?" Martin said finally. "We'll do the simulation as described. But from here on out, every day when we finish our daily route, four members of the ground team will remain behind and take turns practicing landings, takeoffs, and short flights around the area. And, if we are asked to assist the Civil Air Patrol in the search, ground team members will fly with Sally and me as pilots in the two-seat ultralights."

The compromise erased the tension. Karina breathed a deep sigh of relief. Martin and Sally gave them a few more details about the C.A.P. and encouraged them to consider membership after they reached seventeen, the legal age to become licensed as a private pilot. They were told not to expect too much enthusiasm about being asked to help in the search. Many private pilots considered ultralight pilots a notch below them, that is, not quite "real" pilots.

Paul and Jessica headed outside to look over the planes, at least so they said. Jessica's petite build and auburn hair strongly contrasted Paul's lanky frame and sun-bleached hair. Karina knew they were becoming an item. She wondered what parts of the planes they would to be checking.

Megan left with Katie, leaving Karina and Joe alone in the small hangar they used for a classroom while at the Oshkosh airport. Everyone else, including the instructors, had departed earlier. The pilots had been told to turn in early, for tomorrow would be a stressful day.

"Good luck," Joe said, sliding his arm around Karina.

She made a quick search around the room, rose up on tip-toes, placed a small kiss on Joe's lips, and said, "I'm going to win tomorrow, so don't get any ideas otherwise."

Karina ducked under Joe's arm as he tried to return the kiss. She shoved him aside and headed for the door, stopping only long enough to make sure Joe was following.

"Wait till I get my hands on you." Joe chased her from the building.

Karina ran behind the building and across the field toward the hangars. She saw Megan and Katie standing in the hangar doorway and signaled to them. Joe chased, and his longer legs closed the distance, but he couldn't see the other two girls because Karina was blocking his view. He caught her just outside the hangar, penned her to the hangar wall, dropped a quick kiss on her forehead, and said, "You're a great pilot, but I'm better, so don't get your hopes up."

Karina took his hand and walked through the hangar door, speaking loudly, "Don't bet on it. Girls rule and boys drool."

Just inside the door, Karina ducked as Megan and Katie let fly with two bucketfuls of water and deluged Joe.

All three girls rolled on the hangar floor, laughing hysterically. Startled, Joe just stood there at first. Then, he started laughing, too.

They sat down on the bare cement floor and talked until dark. On that warm, June day, they found themselves bonded together by the remaining journey that must still be completed, the next day's competition, and friendships that crossed all boundaries. Whatever the next day brought, they would be friends forever. That had kind of sneaked up on them. The tension from Katie's challenge had bonded them closer than even the events of the cross-country flight. Win, lose, or draw, they would take each day as it came.

* * *

Karina finished brushing her teeth, noting once again that some day she was going to need braces. She padded barefoot across thick carpet. Plush fiber squished between her toes as she crossed to her bed. She was fortunate to have a room and bed all to herself. Each student involved in tomorrow's competition was provided a room for his or her own private use. It was the first time since leaving Mitchum Field that Karina had such privacy.

She got into bed, said her prayers and quietly watched wispy cotton-like clouds decorate the full moon hanging just outside her window. Her thoughts drifted to her parents. Funny, this was the first time she had thought about her parents in days.

Karina pushed away the light sheet covering her, slid out of bed, and inched her way across the moonlit room to her backpack resting in the wicker rocking chair opposite the bed. She opened the secret pouch inside the top flap and removed a small silver locket. It was the only earthly possession she had from her parents. Inside were two small pictures. On one side was a picture of her mother and father, and on the other was a picture of eight-year-old Karina sitting on her father's lap and holding onto her mother's hand. It had been taken just one month before the accident. A portrait, once meant to be a keepsake, was now the only link Karina had left.

She fastened the locket's chain around her neck and inched back to bed. Climbing in, she decided it was too hot to sleep under covers. Karina opened the little locket again and lay in bed at an angle where the moonlight streaming in through the window illuminated the small pictures inside. A refreshing flower-scented breeze blew in through the screened window. Karina tried to recall as many memories of her parents as possible.

"Be with me tomorrow, Papa," Karina said. Tears blurred her vision of her strong, handsome father, with his arms around one of the most beautiful, caring ladies in the world, her mother.

"Tomorrow is for you," she whispered.

Karina's last memory was that of glowing white moonlight silhouetting her parents. *Almost like angels*, she thought.

Chapter 7

Lost and Found

"Any further questions?" Martin asked.

Everyone remained quiet, lost in thought, anxiously waiting. For the past hour, they had reviewed every detail, every procedure. The planes had been checked over, fueled, and prepared for flight. Everything was ready.

"Then, let's hit it," Martin said to dismiss the group.

Karina wished everyone good luck, but she really hoped everyone's luck was slightly less than hers. She donned her flight suit, put on her helmet and adjusted her radio headset microphone. She heard Paul already requesting permission for takeoff.

They joined Martin, the ground team, and other curious spectators on the side of the runway, just in time to see the landing attempt. Paul came in a little high and drifted over the landing mark. He quickly flared the plane's nose up, but missed the mark by more than twenty yards.

"Good luck." Karina hugged Megan, and then crossed her fingers behind her back. "Looks like Paul left the gate wide open."

Megan ran to replace Paul in *Jet Stream*. She taxied the sleek little ultralight down the runway, turned around, and lifted off into a bright, cloudless sky. Paul came grumbling to the group, kicking the ground as he walked.

"Can't believe I missed it by that much," Paul said to Joe. "Gotta be careful. Those two-seat planes come in a lot quicker and glide farther. I've spent too much time in the singles."

Karina noted Paul's comments. She promised herself that she wouldn't make the same mistake. Landings were supposed to be her specialty, but Paul had a point. She had not flown in one of the two-seat ultralights since the journey had begun.

Megan made her run. She came in low and flared more smoothly than Paul had. When the wheels finally touched down and she braked the plane to a halt, Megan landed just short of the mark, a little less than ten feet. That would be a hard score to beat.

"Good luck," said Jessica, who was scheduled for the last attempt. She patted Karina on the back.

"Yeah," Joe said. "Show us how these things work."

Karina smiled, hugged Jessica and Joe, and jogged to *Jet Stream*. Megan handed her the ignition key, smiled and wished her luck.

"Watch the wind sock," Megan said. "A sudden crosswind nearly pushed me away from the runway, about twenty yards out."

"I will, thanks. You set a mark that will be hard to beat," said Karina.

She climbed into *Jet Stream*, fastened her seat belt and shoulder harness and requested permission for takeoff. Following Megan's suggestion, she scrutinized the windsock and zoomed down the runway.

She had no trouble at all on takeoff. The wind remained steady, and the plane lifted effortlessly into a clear blue sky. Karina climbed to 2800-feet, the pattern altitude for this airport, and made the transition from climbing to level flight.

She turned left and began her downwind run. Karina could see the mark clearly from this altitude. A large white cloth "X" had been taped onto the center of the runway about a hundred feet from the west end.

"Turning crosswind. Over," she said into her microphone. It wasn't necessary to speak, but Karina wanted everyone keeping pace with her. She planned to put on a show and demonstrate the perfect way to set an ultralight down where she wanted it to land.

Karina made a flawless upwind final approach and began her descent. She cut her airspeed and noted her rate of descent. Karina lined up on the cloth "X" and tried to make sure that she was coming in at the correct angle. She set the plane down about 80-feet in front of the "X", applied the brakes, and pulled to a stop only three feet from its center.

"Nice going," Joe said, lifting Karina out of the ultralight. "You really set a mark to shoot for."

"Told you so," Karina said. But, she wished Joe luck anyway and trotted over to hug Megan and Jessica while Joe clambered into *Jet Stream* and took off.

"Nice landing," Martin said. "It's going to raise the intensity level."

However, Karina's excitement faded to obscurity just minutes later as Joe made a remarkable landing, stopping only a foot and a half short of the "X's" centerline. Karina's mouth dropped open, and her face must have reflected her dismay because everyone tried to console her—everyone except Joe.

Joe excitedly jumped up and down, letting out an Indian war whoop. He picked Karina up and swung her around before he noticed her crestfallen expression.

"Oh, Karina. I'm sorry, but I just had to," Joe said.

"It's okay. I'm okay." Karina nurtured a smile. "Besides, Jessica can still come through."

Karina turned and noticed Megan standing apart from the group, and her heart went out to the girl who had become such a close friend. She shoved her own disappointment aside and went to stand beside Megan.

Karina reassuringly took Megan's hand in her own and gave it a firm squeeze, receiving a weak smile in return.

Karina understood why Megan was not enticed by Jessica's attempt. She was out either way. If Jessica won, Karina and Jessica would be the pilots. If Joe's score held up, he and Paul would be flying the C.A.P. mission. Still, Karina noticed that Megan was a good trooper and followed every movement the ultralight made. Everyone held his or her breath watching Jessica vault up into the sky.

Coming in above the hangars, Jessica wobbled a little left, and then right. Uplift from the redirected wind startled her a bit. Through the ultralight's windshield, Karina could see Jessica concentrating so fully on her landing mark that she had forgotten about the fundamentals of landing over buildings.

Flaring out into a controlled stall, Jessica set down close to the mark, braked hard, and stopped on top of the "X". The boys groaned, and the girls rushed to the plane, hoisted Jessica from the cockpit and carried her on their shoulders to the side of the runway. Megan climbed in and taxied *Jet Stream* to the hangar.

"Like we said yesterday, girls rule and boys drool," Jessica said, but Paul and Joe took it in stride. Everyone, including Sally and Martin, were pleased with her. Of the students participating in the test, Jessica's landing ability was usually third behind Joe's and Karina's. She excelled in everything else: avionics, takeoffs, turns, stalls, navigation and formation flying. However, landings baffled her. Jessica thought she might have a problem with depth perception.

"Congratulations and condolences." Martin pushed through the excited young people. "Jessica will pilot and Karina will ride as passenger. You two," he said to Karina and Jessica, "head to the briefing room. We have a lot of details to tie up before you depart this afternoon."

Martin's words hushed the crowd. They hadn't realized the exercise would begin so soon. The town was throwing a barbecue that afternoon, followed by an evening dance.

Jessica and Karina could have cared less. They were the chosen, and they were ready for anything. They'd be willing to give up a hundred evenings of dances and parties for this chance to prove themselves. The two girls strolled to the briefing room, arm in arm.

Martin entered and found the girls scrutinizing maps of the area. "Good. I like the way you're taking this seriously." He pulled down a wall map that was much larger than the foldout maps Karina and Jessica were reviewing.

"Where are we headed?" Jessica asked.

"Winona." Martin pointed to a small town located on the map. "You may land in any public field from here to here." Martin traced a line from Oshkosh to Winona.

"How about—." Karina began.

"Whoa, don't say another word," Martin said. "Sally will join us in a few minutes, and you can discuss landing possibilities with her. She is the only one who is supposed to know the area where you set down. However, she'll inform me if the need arises."

Martin grabbed a clipboard from one of the long metal shelves lining the hangar's metal wall. "Your protocol is this. You will identify a safe area in which to land." He turned to Jessica. "Before even considering a landing, check with Sally for clearance. Understand?"

"Yes, sir. Perfectly," she said. "Where is Sally?"

"She's loading the necessary equipment into *Blue Bird*," Martin said. "She should be here any minute now."

"What equipment?" Karina asked.

"A two-day supply of food and water, blankets, and a small CD player to help pass the time," Martin said. "Also, some makeup to transform you into crash victims."

"What type of injuries?" Jessica asked.

"You will have a broken leg, broken collarbone, and severe head injury," Martin said to her. Then he turned to Karina. "Karina, you will be conscious, but have a possible broken back and a compound fracture of the left leg above the knee. When discovered, you will still be in the plane. Jessica will be on the ground outside."

Sally entered, carrying a couple of ponchos and two small backpacks. "Hi, guys. I've got some insect repellent and toiletries for you plus a few other surprises. Don't open these until after you're settled in for the night."

"You don't think they'll find us before dark?" asked Karina.

Martin said, "The C.A.P. will probably not receive notification until a little before dark, so chances are you will have at least one night at the crash site."

"What if they don't find us?" asked Jessica. "How will we know when it's all right to return?"

"The C.A.P. is a pretty efficient organization. They have some really good pilots and lots of experience at search and rescue, so they should be able to find you within 24- to 36-hours," said Martin. "Just lay low and wait it out. Here is a cell phone you can use in case there are any unexpected problems."

Martin handed the phone to Karina and ordered her to keep it in the plane with her. The remaining details were quickly worked out. Martin took them to lunch, not to a fast-food joint, but to a real restaurant.

Martin said to order whatever they wanted. Karina and Jessica took him at his words. Karina ordered steak and lobster with a baked potato, vegetables, and a garden salad. Jessica order crab legs and a shrimp platter, consisting of shrimp prepared three different ways. Everyone was so stuffed by the end of the meal that they had to pass on dessert. Martin promised them ice cream sundaes after the exercise ended. Afterwards, the girls took showers and had a short nap. Takeoff time was scheduled for four-thirty in the afternoon.

* * *

"See anything promising?" Jessica banked the plane left to give Karina a better view of the ground. Below lay rolling hills covered with trees. Most open fields were filled with crops of corn or soybeans.

They had been in the air for almost an hour, but hadn't found anyplace intriguing to set down. At best, they would have another hour to find a location. After that, they wouldn't have enough fuel to return to Oshkosh. The plane was a little heavy, loaded with extra weight from the supplies stored underneath the seats.

"Let's try the park. Maybe we can find an open area there," said Karina. She felt uneasy and tense, though she wasn't sure why. Maybe it was because she was along as a passenger, or because the wind had picked up during the early afternoon and was bouncing them around. Either way, Karina wanted to find a place to set down. She wanted to get the exercise started.

"What's the heading?" Jessica leveled the plane and started a slow turn to the right.

"Two—four—zero degrees. The park should be on your left about ten miles out. If it has a spot large enough to set down, it should be a good test for the C.A.P. We'd be almost twenty miles west of our flight plan." Karina directed Jessica toward the state park.

The plane suddenly hit a downdraft and dropped about fifty feet. "Whoa, look out! You okay?" Jessica asked.

"I'm okay." Karina forced the words through clenched teeth. Her knuckles went white from the death grip she had on her seat. She couldn't force herself to say more. Closing her eyes, she swallowed the cold metallic taste of fear rising in her throat. *Please,* she pleaded silently, *don't let me lose it up here.* Inside, she trembled uncontrollably.

"Hey, how about there?" Jessica put the plane in a 20-degree banking turn to the left. "Next to the lake, the field on that little knoll? It's short, but if we can get in there, it should give the C.A.P. fits trying to find us."

"Looks perfect." Karina forced her hands to release their desperate hold from the seat and willed her breathing to normal. "Do a slow flight over the area and check with Sally."

"*Blue Bird* to *Jet Stream*," Jessica radioed Sally. "How about that field on the hill near the lake, about a thousand yards out? Over."

"I don't see it. Over," came Sally's response.

"Small field at your two o'clock," Jessica said. "Looks deserted and nobody's on the lake at this end. Over."

"Pretty short. Do you think there's enough clearance for takeoff afterwards? Over." Sally asked.

Karina broke into the conversation, "Once we're down and rescued, the plane can be pushed out. See that dirt wagon road running from the blacktop? We could lift off from there, and such a tight landing site should make it difficult for the C.A.P. to locate us. I don't see any campsites or other structures nearby. Over."

"Good thinking," Sally said. "You two stay up and let me take a once-around. Over."

Karina and Jessica circled at 1500-feet while Sally set up for a landing and did a flyby. The field looked like an old baseball park. Everything had been cut down and cleared away. The field appeared slightly slanted and was surrounded by tall trees. It was hard to tell if there were any large ruts to worry about.

"Looks to be about a hundred and fifty yards long and a little less than a hundred yards wide," Sally informed them. "With those trees surrounding the field, you'll have to go in steep and flare out immediately. Sure you want to try it? Over."

"I think we can handle it," Jessica said after consulting with Karina. "If we've got an okay, we're ready to start. Over."

After a tense pause, Sally said, "You're cleared to land. Be safe and good luck. Over."

Karina held her breath for what seemed like the hundredth time while Jessica started her descent. The girls noticed ripples on the west end of the lake, indicating the wind direction at ground level. It seemed strong enough to give them the lift needed for a short field flare out.

Jessica brought the ultralight down, just clearing the trees, cut her power, and brought the plane's nose up in a perfect flare out. The ultralight's back wheels came down first, and the plane skimmed across the field.

For a moment, Karina thought they were going to end up in the trees, but the little two-seat plane rolled to a stop thirty yards from any danger. Both girls breathed a deep sigh of relief.

"Nice going," Karina said to Jessica, patting her friend's helmet.

"*Blue Bird* down. Beginning exercise. Over," Jessica radioed Sally.

"Nice landing. See you guys in a day or so," Sally said through their headsets. "Returning to base. Enjoy. Over."

They opened the canopy. Necks craned to the sky, they watched *Jet Stream* become a small speck and disappear. Then, the girls climbed out and pushed the plane under cover of a strand of tall oak trees until only a small section of tail remained visible. The spot was perfect. A deep rut just inside the woods let them put the plane's nose down, which raised the tail. Anyone looking from above, when they were finally spotted, would think that they had gone in nose first.

After the plane was positioned to their satisfaction, Karina pulled a small sack from underneath the rear seat. Martin had instructed her to open it once they were settled. She slung the sack over her shoulder and inched her way to the ground. With the plane's tail in the air, she had to tiptoe just to reach the ground.

The sack contained a first aid book, makeup scar wax, fake blood, instructions on how to produce artificial wounds and other trauma necessities. Karina laid them out, and the girls giggled their way through creating fabulous wounds. Karina pulled up a pant leg and applied some scar wax to her thigh, near one of her real scars. Then, she took a chicken bone that had been supplied, dried and cleaned, and placed it into the wax, smoothing it over until just the tip protruded. Jessica helped by finding some dirt and darkening the wax and Karina's leg until it was almost impossible to separate real flesh from fake skin. It took nearly two hours, but the girls made themselves up quite professionally. While doing so, the sun made a slow arc across the western sky.

"Think they're looking for us yet?" Jessica asked, moving into her position next to the "crashed" plane.

Karina, positioned in the back seat of the plane, glanced at her watch. "Maybe, maybe not. We've probably been reported overdue, but I don't know how fast they can send planes to look for us. It'll be dark soon."

"Karina?" Jessica asked tentatively. "Those nightmares you had when you first came to Blue Horizons, do they have anything to do with those scars on your legs?"

Karina sat silent, summoning courage to answer Jessica. She didn't really want to talk about the accident. In fact, for the first time since she could remember, the nightmares had been pushed into the deep recesses of her mind. They no longer consumed her every waking moment. Oh, that didn't mean she had completely forgotten them. When she let her guard down, they came rushing back. But at least they no longer dominated her every feeling and every action.

"I'm sorry," Jessica said. "You don't have to answer if you don't want to talk about it. Just before you came, Martin told us that you had been in an accident that had killed your parents. It was foolish of me to bring it up."

"It's okay." Karina spoke slowly, guarding against the flood of emotions that built inside her every time she tried to talk about the fateful event that had so tragically altered her life. "It happened when I was eight. My father was flying us over the mountains of Kyrgyzstan in a small plane when we got caught in a sudden thunderstorm. The plane's radio wasn't working, like most Russian technology at the time. We didn't even know a storm was building until it hit. It came from the other side of the mountains. Father couldn't find a place to land before the clouds closed in and reduced visibility to almost zero."

Karina's voice tightened further with each memory, anger welling inside her. Anger that she had never been fully able to control. Without warning, she smashed her fist against the seat in front of her, startling Jessica, who jumped in surprise, painfully ramming an elbow against a wing strut.

"Stop," Jessica said, rubbing her throbbing elbow. "Please. Don't say more. I don't want you angry with me. Forget I asked."

Karina sighed. She knew her sudden anger had frightened Jessica. "Sorry. I'm not angry at you, or anyone, for that matter. Strange, when I think about the accident, I get furious all over again, sometimes without even knowing it. It happened so long ago, but I still can't seem to control the anger, and I don't know who I'm angry with. Maybe myself for surviving."

Jessica crawled into the front seat of the plane, ignoring the fact that she was supposed to have a head injury. Reaching around the seat, she took hold of Karina's hand. "Karina, you've got to be the bravest person I know. Martin told us that your parents were killed in an accident, but we had no idea it was a plane crash."

Karina felt the tears sliding down her face. "Brave? I can't even handle a nightmare."

"Think about it," Jessica said. "Getting into a small plane, overcoming the nightmares, and flying across the United States in a plane put together by a mixed-up band of misfits whose parents don't even want them has got to be somewhere in the definition of brave. It probably borders on fearless."

The roar of a low-flying airplane interrupted the girls before Karina could respond to Jessica's last remark. It flew directly over the girls, heading into the setting sun. The sound died away, only to return from another direction, leaving little doubt that it was searching for them.

Jessica scampered over the side and dropped prostrate onto the ground. Face down with one arm underneath her, she pretended to be unconscious. Karina slunk lower into the seat and rested her head against the left side of the plane. Hearts racing, they waited for the expected rescue.

The search plane made a thorough sweep of the area, but in dim twilight, near the end of a warm summer day, there wasn't enough light to see a three-foot tail section camouflaged in the shadows of a setting sun. The girls waited patiently until an hour after dark.

"Hey, do you think I can move now?" Jessica called up to Karina, wiggling her legs to discourage hovering mosquitoes. "These lousy mosquitoes are eating me alive."

"Sure," Karina said, shifting to better see her friend. "It's too dark for anyone to see us from the air. We might as well make ourselves comfortable."

Jessica climbed into the narrow cockpit, and the girls settled in for the night. If a land search was being made for them, they should have some warning before rescuers got to them, and if not, they would just ad lib.

Karina popped open cans of cold Pepsi that Sally had stored in a basket beneath the front seat, and the girls dined on cold Kentucky Fried Chicken and potato salad. It was the last "real food" they would have until a rescue party delivered them from this exercise. From here on, it would be pretzels, snacks and bottled water.

The night passed slowly, providing the girls with ample opportunity for talk, and talk they did. First, Jessica talked about her parents and how they were too busy for her. Then, they discussed boys. After which, Karina filled Jessica in on the events that had led her to Blue Horizons, which Jessica didn't believe at first because she couldn't imagine Karina stealing anything. Then, they discussed boys, school, future hopes and goals, and finished with more discussion about boys.

Karina outlasted Jessica and sat for a long time listening to her friend's rhythmic breathing. She'd hidden it well from Jessica, but Karina was still angry, deep down angry. She wanted to get out of the plane, scream, kick and shout her lungs out.

Will I ever get over this domineering anger? How can I ever lead a normal life if reason can't control raw emotion?

The accident had happened so long ago and was clouded in her memory. Yet in the dark dredges of sleep, it conjured up from her very soul nightmares so vivid as to be current reality and an irresistible force. Until she learned to deal with those internal torments, Karina would never find peace.

Overtaken by sleep, her final memories once more carried her to that fateful night. Instinctively, her legs pushed against the front seat. Jessica stirred briefly. Karina shifted position, and settled into an uncomfortable dream about crash landing into the middle of a dense forest.

* * *

Hours later, as the sun began chasing darkness from the forest, a rustling noise plucked Karina from restless sleep. It came from behind her. What could it be? Jessica stirred from the front seat. Something was moving directly behind Karina, low and inside the plane.

"What's that?" asked Jessica in an anxious, sleep-labored voice. "Have they found us? I've got to get onto the ground?"

"No. Wait," Karina whispered. "I think something's in here with us, just behind my seat. You don't think a snake could have dropped down from the trees above us? I shouldn't have left the canopy open."

Karina inched her legs underneath her, so she could turn around, spy on whatever was behind her seat, and perhaps make a hasty exit. Peering over the top of the seat, she found herself staring at the face of a furry black-masked bandit. She giggled, and the startled raccoon darted over the side and vanished into the shadowy forest.

"What is it?" Jessica asked. Karina was blocking her view. "What's so funny?"

"We've been robbed." Karina laughed, hauling their ravaged food sack over the seat. She turned and faced her bewildered friend. "We've just been held up by a raccoon. Man, it devastated our food supply. What hasn't been eaten, has been picked through."

The girls realized how hungry they were and bemoaned their luck. Only three Hostess fruit pies and a Hershey's chocolate bar with almonds remained unmolested from the clutches of their unwelcome guest.

Eating slowly, savoring each morsel, the girls finished their meager breakfast, drank half of their remaining water supply, and decided that being rescued early would be in their own best interests.

In that respect, they were lucky. Not long after they finished breakfast and slipped into the cover of a dense strand of woods that they used for their bathroom, the girls heard the distant roar of a propeller-driven airplane approaching from the direction of the lake.

"There." Karina pointed. "Better get ready. You don't want to be seen standing."

Jessica, who was standing beside the plane, dropped to her well-practiced position just seconds before the Cessna passed low overhead. This time, instead of flying off to begin another pattern search, the small plane began circling slowly around the field. Then, once more, it made a low sweep over the field.

"Think they've seen us, yet?" Jessica asked Karina, who had slumped forward in her seat, head resting against the side of the ultralight. "I can't see anything from this position."

"I don't know," said Karina with her mouth pressed against the front seat. "I can't see anything either, but I think they're circling again."

Less than five minutes later, while the plane alternated between circling and making passes above the short tree-lined grass field hiding them, the girls heard the rising wail of a siren. Soon, a ground rescue team surrounded them.

Later that evening, Martin informed Karina and Jessica that once the plane had been spotted, the rescue team was informed that the emergency was an exercise; however, they had treated the girls as if the crash and resulting injuries were real.

The rescue crew, consisting of a sheriff's deputy, young ambulance crew, and two C.A.P. members, first checked to make sure that both

Jessica and Karina were alive and breathing. The sheriff's deputy and C.A.P. team worked on Jessica, while the ambulance crew tended Karina.

"I can't feel my legs." She gasped as one of the young men began evaluating her condition. Karina decided to give them a show. "How's Jessie? I haven't heard from her since the crash. Is she dead? Please, tell me she's not dead."

"Your friend is unconscious, but alive," the kind young man answered in a gentle, soothing manner. He prodded and probed all over Karina, constantly speaking in that low, soothing monotone.

The young man couldn't have been more than twenty-two, she decided as he finally raised her head and immobilized it with a retractable neck brace that fastened to the backboard, which had already been slipped in behind her.

Karina could see Jessica being lifted onto a stretcher, an IV taped to her arm. She couldn't see if the rescue team had actually inserted the IV needle into Jessica's arm. She certainly hoped they weren't taking this exercise that seriously. Karina hated needles.

"Okay, miss," the young man said, his slightly older partner at his side. "We're going to lift you out now. When that happens, your legs are going to straighten out. Let us know immediately if there is any pain, any pain at all. Understand?"

Karina would have nodded, except for the restraints that bound her head, holding it immobile. "Yes, sir. Right now, I can't feel a thing, but my leg's bleeding again."

"We'll take care of that as soon as you're out," the kind voice said. "Here we go."

They lifted her out and gently lowered her to the ground. Immediately, one of the young men immobilized her with restraining straps across the forehead and chest while the other rescuer cut her pant leg from ankle to hip.

Karina almost blurted for him to stop when she felt air blowing over her bare leg. She could imagine her underpants with white cotton lace exposed to public view. She was just about to inform these guys that they were taking this exercise a little too seriously, but they slipped a pressure bandage over her "bone fragment," applied an air splint, and covered her embarrassment with a blanket before she could summon up the courage to interfere.

"Hey, those are my good pants," was all Karina could get out.

This brought a smile from the older rescuer. "Don't worry. You'll get a voucher for a brand-new pair when we get you back and you're declared well."

"That is, if you're alive and well," said the younger man to tease her.

Siren screaming, the ambulance transported Karina and Jessica to a local trauma center where their simulated injuries were diagnosed and treated. An hour later, they were pronounced well, and the exercise was over. After a slight shopping spree to replace the clothes ruined in the exercise, Sally and Martin drove them to Oshkosh to a surprise party.

Everyone wanted to know what had happened, and Joe was more than a little miffed with Karina's details about the rescue, especially the part about her two young rescuers. Karina highly exaggerated the cutting of her pants and was pleased to see Joe flush with jealousy.

After a delicious meal of barbecued hamburgers, corn on the cob, baked potatoes and ice cream sundaes, Martin informed the group that it was time they got some sleep. Tomorrow, he informed them, they would fly southwest, down through Illinois headed toward Missouri, the "Show Me" state.

That night, watching TV with her host family, Karina noticed a changing weather pattern. They might be in for some rough flying ahead. A hurricane named Caesar was moving north into the Gulf Coast and was expected to send a lot of rain upward throughout the Midwest. She certainly hoped this weather pattern wouldn't ground them for any length of time. She was beginning to like all the attention the trip was providing.

Brushing tangles from her freshly dried hair before slipping under her covers, Karina took a long look at herself in the round mirror hanging above the antique wooden dressing table next to her bed. She appeared the same—same slender build, same shoulder-length reddish brown hair, and same green eyes—but inside she somehow felt different. What she and Jessica had done during the past two days had changed her. She wasn't sure what change had occurred, but she felt all tingly inside. The thought that Joe was jealous of a rescue worker and the feeling of accomplishment at helping in the rescue exercise excited her. She wondered how successfully completing this trip would make her feel.

Karina finished her self-examination and belly-flopped across the bed. Snuggling with her pillow, she reminisced about events from the previous 48-hours. Sleep captured her with an image of Joe's slightly flushed face imploring her to say no more about her rescue.

Chapter 8

Turbulence

"*Lady Bird* calling *Meadow Lark*. Hey, Karina, see that wall of clouds over there at two o'clock? Aren't those stratus clouds?" Megan said to Karina over her headset. "That means smooth flying, doesn't it? Over."

Karina looked to her right. They passed directions to each other as if a clock had been laid down and they were in the center of it. Twelve o'clock was directly in front; three o'clock was straight off to the right, so two o'clock was in-between, at about sixty degrees. However, to her dismay, the clouds she spied were not stratus clouds, a good indicator of smooth air.

"I see them," Karina said to Megan, "but those aren't strati. They're cumuli. Looks like we might be in for a rough ride. Over."

Cumulus clouds, which built into mighty, anvil-topped cumulonimbus thunderstorm clouds, still held terror for Karina. Her mouth felt like cotton again, and her hands were sweating on the control stick. They were only halfway to their scheduled stop at Fulton, Missouri, and few places along the route provided adequate emergency landing sites.

Unlike many places in Illinois, which were flat, treeless farmland, this part of Missouri was mostly small farms and tree-covered hills. Ever since the students had crossed the Mississippi and Missouri Rivers and worked their way south of Interstate Highway 70, they'd had fewer and fewer places to land. At the moment, they were high above colorful rolling, tree-covered hills. If forced to land quickly, they'd have to choose between landing on a road or on one of the small fence-lined fields surrounded by high trees, a tricky maneuver at best.

The massive wall of billowy white clouds looked beautiful from a distance, but Karina knew the danger. Built up during daytime heat, convection currents caused turbulence and updrafts that could suck the ultralights into the clouds. The winds inside those clouds could rip the wings off a small plane or suddenly lift it thousands of feet into the air. Cumulonimbus clouds could top out above 50,000 feet, far above the ability of a person to survive in an unpressurized cockpit.

Karina remembered a story from her literature book that told about an air force pilot who ejected from his plane in a thunderstorm. He was tossed up and down for over an hour before a lucky wind gust released him from his torment. He had been extremely lucky. Karina had no intention of leaving her fate to luck.

"*Blue Bird* calling *Jet Stream*, do you copy? Over." Sally's call interrupted Karina's thoughts, enabling her to take a deep breath and loosen her grip on the control stick.

"I copy," said Martin. "I see them. I figure we still have a couple of hours before the situation becomes critical. That storm front is building slowly, and we're only about an hour from Fulton. We may have a bumpy ride at the end and some crosswind, but I think we should keep on course and make for the Fulton airport. If we can't make it that far, there's a small ultralight field just north of Fulton that we can try for. Over."

Karina keyed her microphone. "Martin, what happens if the wind picks up? Shouldn't we set down before we have too much wind? Over." She found her voice shaking as she spoke and hoped nobody else noticed.

"We should be far enough ahead of the storm to make it down safely," Martin answered. "Hold it together, Karina. You're doing fine. We shouldn't have more than a bumpy ride to contend with, and I assure you, if the situation changes, we'll set down at the first safe spot. The ground team has picked out three fields that will do in an emergency. They're on your kneeboard. Remember? Over."

"Yes, sir. Over," she mumbled between clenched teeth.

Her heart raced again, pounding so hard she could hear it echoing in her headset. Karina felt fear and anger overtaking her. She wanted down, and she wanted down immediately. A few months ago, she would have just set the plane down at the first available space large enough for a safe landing and taken the consequences. Maybe she would yet. However, Karina had developed a sort of loyalty to Martin and the rest of the kids. She didn't want to let them down.

"Karina!" Martin's voice was sharp. "Watch your altitude. Keep your mind on business. Over."

While confronting her fear, Karina hadn't noticed that her plane had begun a slow descent. Perhaps, it was her subconscious taking over, allowing the little plane to lose almost 300-feet. She gently pulled the control stick and regained the lost altitude, up to 2200-feet above ground level, their cruising altitude for this leg of the trip.

Martin began a dialog with her and the other kids to ease frayed nerves. They rehearsed emergency procedures, how to land on a short field, a soft field, and fields with a control tower, anything to keep their minds away from the storm clouds building around them. Still, the turbulence increased, and so did the number and size of clouds in the area.

Nearing the town of Fulton, Missouri, they were being bounced around like a rag doll in a running child's arms. Fulton's airport was small, consisting of two runways: one concrete and one grass.

Karina was supposed to land third because that was her flight position for the day, but Martin instructed her to move up and land directly behind Sally. Normally, she would have been offended at being given special consideration, but today Karina simply increased power and moved in behind Sally.

After Sally landed and taxied off of the concrete runway, Karina nosed her plane down. Heavy breathing made her a little dizzy. She lined up on the runway, coming in at an angle steep enough to be considered a dive.

"Karina," Martin said. "Pull up, go around, and try again. I said abort your landing! Do as I say! Over." Martin practically yelled into his microphone.

Karina wasn't listening. Her eyes saw only the runway, rapidly approaching, filling her windshield. Rational thinking was beyond her. All she wanted was to be down and safely out of the plane. Her hands worked the stick and her eyes were fixed on the runway, but her mind took her to that other storm, the one that took her parents from her, the one that left her empty inside, except for the nightmares and anger. She was coming in too steep, too fast, and would have crashed straight into the runway, but a voice other than Martin's, a vaguely familiar voice, took command.

"Karina," said Joe's voice pleasantly, with no hint of anxiety. "Kill your power and flare out. I'm right behind you. Listen to me. You can do this. It's just routine. Flare out now. Over."

Trembling violently, she did as Joe said just before hitting the pavement. The little plane responded quickly but was traveling too fast to make efficient use of ground effect. Her main wheels hit hard, and the plane bounced back up into the air. She glided along for another hundred feet before touching down again, this time with less force than the time before. The ultralight stayed on the ground, but it leaned oddly to the right as it rolled to the end of the runway.

Karina pushed up the canopy, leaned her head outside the cockpit, and vomited. Her legs wouldn't move, and she sat crying with her head in her lap until Joe and Martin half-pulled, half-lifted her from the plane. She pulled herself together enough to make it inside the small white building that served as a control tower. Fortunately, the bathroom was empty. Unfortunately, so was her stomach and the dry heaves were sickening.

Afterwards, Karina was a basket case, crying out of control. She didn't speak to anyone, and couldn't stop crying and shaking.

The rest of the group landed safely, and the ground team battened down everything before the thunderstorm hit in force. For over an hour and a half, buckets of rain fell from the sky, and the wind howled like an injured monster from one of those old Japanese horror films. Karina hardly noticed. She was lost in her own world, her own nightmare. Her tears lasted longer than the storm, and she barely remembered being moved to the van and bedded down on the back seat underneath a pile of sleeping bags. Nor did she remember Jessica and Sally sitting beside her, holding her hand, giving her as much comfort as possible.

* * *

"I'm not sure what happened up there yesterday, Karina," Martin said. "But until we get it sorted out, you're grounded. Didn't you hear me tell you to abort your landing and go around for another attempt?"

Karina could tell Martin was really upset with her. This was not just Martin's angry response when someone didn't listen—this was serious. A day earlier, his grounding her would have been a horrendous punishment, but right now she didn't care if she ever got back into those torture machines. And she wasn't open to any discussion about it.

"I don't remember hearing anything," she said slowly, deliberately. "Ground me all you like. I'm never getting into a plane again, of any kind."

"We'll see about that later," Martin eyed her up and down. "For now, you'll work with Valerie on the ground and do some public relations work. You will be polite, on time, and in bed by nine o'clock. Understand?" Martin's voice had a threatening hint to it, daring Karina to respond, to challenge.

Being sent to bed early was a stiff punishment; every kid at Blue Horizons hated it. However, at the moment, Karina could care less. She just wanted out of there. She'd do anything, but agree to fly again, anything to stay out of the air.

"Yes, sir." She nodded and said nothing else.

Martin continued staring at her, and it made her uncomfortable. Why didn't he get on with it and let her go? She shifted weight to her other foot and met his stare without flinching. They stood staring for an eternity, neither speaking nor looking away. Each measured the other, looking for a weakness to exploit, leverage with which to gain an upper hand, to be in control.

Finally, Martin broke the deadlock. "I've arranged for you to stay with a family in town while we're here. With the current developing weather system, we may be here a few days, maybe longer. They have an eleven-year-old daughter and need someone to sit with her during the day. You might even be able to earn a little spending money."

Karina was caught off guard by this turn of events. "What about classes?"

"You can bring the child with you," Martin said. "She loves flying. Hanging around us ought to excite her."

Karina shrugged. "Sure, why not? Can I go now?"

"There's one more thing you should know." Martin waited until he was sure Karina was listening. "Penelope, the little girl you'll be babysitting, has a serious illness. Leukemia. She must be taken to the hospital for treatment twice a week, so treat her kindly."

Karina slumped into a chair, the world spinning around her. For a moment, she thought she would faint. She put her head into her lap, hands on her head.

Martin was beside her, hand on her shoulder to make sure she didn't fall out of the chair. "Relax and control your breathing. Don't sit up yet. Just rest."

Long seconds later, she raised her head. Martin handed her a glass of water and helped her to her feet. Karina wasn't sure why his announcement had such an effect on her. She was still shaky when she climbed into the van's front passenger seat next to Sally.

A short drive to Kingdom City brought Karina to a large white farmhouse surrounded by a yellow picket fence. Gravel crunched underneath tires. Sally braked to a stop.

A blond-haired little girl dressed in a red, white, and blue striped swimsuit burst around the corner of the house and raced to meet them.

"Are you Karina?" she asked. "I'm Penelope, but everyone calls me Penny. Are you going to stay with us? Do you like to swim? We have a swimming pool around back. Did you bring a swimsuit?"

Karina smiled at the steady stream of chatter that didn't allow time for a response.

"I made some brownies this morning," said Penny. "This afternoon, Dad is taking us to St. Louis. I have a doctor's appointment, but afterward we're going to a movie, and then out to eat. What kind of food do you like?"

Karina finally broke into the conversation. "Hold on, girl. Slow down, first things first. My name is Karina. I'm pleased to meet you."

Penny solemnly shook Karina's hand. "I'm so glad you're here. I've been waiting ever since last night when Dad told me that you were coming."

They made their way onto the porch and through the front door. Penny stopped just long enough to grab a towel and wipe off her wet feet. She explained her mother got mad when she tracked water all over the house, and she didn't want to be grounded from the pool now that she had someone to swim with her.

Penny's home was warm and cozy. Hardwood floors, waxed to a shine, ran throughout the house, with area rugs in the dining, living, and family rooms. Large white-framed windows provided ample natural lighting. The walk-through kitchen had a small table sitting next to a Formica-topped serving counter where coffee and conversation would be welcome. The kitchen wasn't arranged for family dining, so Karina assumed the family ate in the dining room.

Upstairs, Karina was led to a beautiful lime green bedroom with white lace curtains. The windows were closed, probably to help keep the air conditioner from having a nervous breakdown. The room was huge. In the middle was a large four-poster bed covered by a cream-colored canopy.

Penny helped Karina settle in, and Sally excused herself, saying that she really had to get back to the airport.

"How long can you stay?" Penny asked, shoving Karina's underwear and socks into a large dresser drawer. "We're going to have a huge fireworks display this year. Can you come?"

"I don't think so." Karina sat on the bed and watched the little girl scramble from one suitcase to the other, obviously content to do everything for her treasured guest. "The Fourth is over a week away. We're leaving as soon as the weather decides what it's going to do."

Penny finished unpacking Karina's skimpy belongings and flopped onto the bed next to her. "You're so lucky. I'd give anything to be a pilot. One day, I'm going to the Air Force Academy at Colorado Springs."

Karina stared at the little girl. If she was ill, she certainly didn't show it, but she had mentioned going to the doctor later in the day. She wondered if Penny knew just how sick she was? Karina decided to change the subject. "Are you here alone? Where are your parents?"

"Oh, Mom's gone to the grocery store and Dad's at work." Penny's bare feet kicked back and forth, almost in rhythm with her words.

"Is your dad out in the fields?" Karina asked. She stood and moved to look out one of the three large windows overlooking the farm.

"Oh, no." Penny giggled. "We inherited the farm. Dad leases the fields to a farmer friend of his. Dad's a pediatrician, a kid doctor. He drives to St. Louis every morning. He works at St. Louis Children's Hospital. It's a long drive, but Dad says it gives him a chance to relax on the way home."

The remainder of that warm June morning, Karina swam with Penny, played cards, and watched Penny's favorite movie, *Fly Away Home*, a movie about a girl who found some geese and learned to fly an ultralight to help them find a place to migrate.

Penny's mother came home and welcomed Karina with a lunch of roast beef sandwiches, fresh-cut cucumbers and tomatoes, corn on the cob, and apple pie for dessert. The short woman had such a warm personality that Karina felt at home almost the instant she was introduced.

Penny's father had to work late, so her mother herded them into the family station wagon and drove them to St. Louis. Penny had to meet her doctor at Cardinal Glennon Children's Hospital for a blood test.

Karina wanted to stay in the waiting room, but couldn't resist Penny's sad little face begging her to come. Karina didn't like hospitals and explained to Mrs. Winfield that she had spent months in a hospital after her accident. This peaked Penny's interest, and she pestered Karina to tell her more, ignoring her own mother's warning looks.

Giving in to Penny's persistence, Karina explained everything in as little detail as possible. At some point during the narration, Penny took Karina's hand. As Karina finished with how she was placed at Blue Horizons, Penny's doctor arrived.

They went into a sparkling white room, and the doctor took three vials of blood from Penny. Penny really liked this doctor and later explained that he was the only doctor she knew who did his own blood work. She had told him years ago that she hated needles, and from that time forward, the doctor took her blood samples himself.

Dr. Winfield, Penny's father, joined them for dinner at an Outback steak house. They had a marvelous meal, saw a movie that starred Robin Williams as a robot trying to become human, and stopped at Ted Drew's, a St. Louis landmark and frozen yogurt monarch.

Both Penny and Karina fell sound asleep during the 90-minute drive home. Penny begged to sleep with Karina, against her mother's objections, and she finally won the battle after Karina said she didn't mind and during this trip had often shared a bed with one of the other kids.

Early the next morning, Karina awoke fully rested. Penny's head was snuggled against her shoulder. The girl, who looked and acted much younger than a child of eleven, was sleeping peacefully. Karina ran fingers through the little girl's long, silky blond hair. She knew Penny was proud of it. Penny had told her how much she had cried when she began treatment for her leukemia and all of her hair had fallen out.

The little girl shifted and Karina put an arm around the child. It just didn't seem fair that such a happy, energetic little girl should face a life-threatening disease. Life just wasn't fair at times, Karina thought. Sleep once again overpowered her.

Rain was falling when the girls finally got up, showered, and headed to breakfast. There would be no flying today, so Karina suggested that Penny go with her to class and then help her prepare the oil-fuel mixture used by the ultralights. She promised to let Penny sit in *Meadow Lark* and assured Mrs. Winfield that Martin wouldn't object.

All day Penny was Karina's shadow. The other kids fussed over her, and Martin didn't even try to restrain them when they drifted into lengthy explanations to Penny's never-ending questions during class lectures.

Rain continued to drum on the metal hangar used as their classroom, so Penny had to settle for sitting in *Meadow Lark* inside the hangar. Karina took a picture with Martin's Polaroid camera and promised Penny another outside, once the weather improved.

The only drag to the day came when Penny learned that Karina had been grounded. Penny had asked if she could snap a picture of Karina taking off when the weather cleared. The question silenced the entire group, and an embarrassed Karina had to explain that she wasn't allowed to fly right now. Karina was angry after that, but valiantly hid it from Penny.

After class, Karina allowed Penny to help her mix fuel for the ultralights. She explained that the engines used on the Challenger ultralights were two-cycle engines and oil had to be mixed directly into the gasoline to protect the engine. Penny hummed happily as she mixed fuel and puttered around the ultralights. She literally beamed when the rain temporarily stopped and Martin placed a flight helmet on her head and packed her into *Jet Stream* for a taxi run up and down the taxiway.

That evening Karina, Penny and her parents played a never-ending game of Monopoly. It was after midnight, long after Karina's curfew, before she went to bed. Only Penny's father, who had surgery early the next morning, went to bed at a respectable hour.

Mrs. Winfield was apologetic for keeping Karina up so late, but Karina brushed that aside. She explained that rain was predicted for tomorrow, so Martin had called off classes until after lunch. The planes were all maintained and ready, so there was little else to do. Secretly, Karina hoped it would rain forever. She felt at home and thoroughly enjoyed how Penny looked up to her. This was the type of family she might have had if not for the accident.

* * *

Three days later, rain still fell steadily. Not only in Missouri, but also throughout the entire Midwest. A series of hurricanes and tropical storms were headed up the Gulf Coast, and this was complicated further by a rainy weather system coming eastward from the Pacific Coast.

During the long lull, Karina caught up with her algebra. Penny's father helped her tremendously. She informed Dr. Winfield that if she passed algebra, he would have her undying gratitude. Mrs. Winfield laughed, and Penny suggested that they adopt Karina, so she could have a sister.

Karina and Penny became very close. So close, in fact, that Penny really opened up to her. She talked about the early days of finding out about her disease, about losing her hair, and about spending days in the hospital. Every night, the two girls slept in Karina's room, cuddled together. Not one time during this period did Karina have a nightmare.

One evening, while Karina sat with Penny to allow Dr. and Mrs. Winfield a night on the town, Penny confided something that forever changed Karina. Penny had just finished her bath, and Karina was shampooing her hair.

"Karina," Penny said. "Want to know my biggest secret?"

"Sure," she said, rinsing shampoo from the child's hair, the pleasant flower-fresh scent filling the entire room.

"I want to fly, to be a pilot," Penny blurted out. "I want to touch the sky, to float like a bird drifting on the wind, free from Earth's bonds. That's my secret wish. I haven't told anyone, not even my parents."

"Tilt your head back. You're going to get shampoo in your eyes," Karina said. "Why don't you tell your dad? He could get you a plane ride. I'm sure he would if you asked him." She squished shampoo from long blond strands.

"No," Penny said quietly. "You don't understand. I want to do this by myself, for me. I know Daddy would give me a ride if I asked. That's just the point. Right now, they do almost anything I ask. I don't want it because I'm dying. I want it because I'm me. I want this for me. I want to be a pilot, just like you."

Karina didn't know what to say. She had never before felt like she did at that moment. Her heart was in her throat, tears dammed back by sheer willpower. She wrung the excess water from Penny's hair and gently guided the fragile girl onto her lap. Using a large white bath towel, Karina briskly rubbed dampness from Penny's silky hair—thus buying her precious seconds to gather composure.

"I'm not much of a pilot. You don't want to be like me," she said finally, rolling the towel turban style around the little girl's head. She turned Penny around. "I'm grounded because I panicked and landed when I wasn't supposed to. I landed hard and bent one of the plane's wheel struts. What's even worse, I placed others in danger because of my fears, my lack of control. I'm not sure I can fly again."

Penny looked at Karina and smiled, a smile that broke Karina's heart, "You can fly. I know you can. You just need confidence. I understand being afraid. When I first got sick, I gave up and almost died. Daddy never left my side. He stayed with me, goaded, nudged, and begged me not to give up. I didn't and here I am."

Penny slid off Karina's lap, hugged her, and streaked from the room dressed only in bath towels. Karina was about to go after her when the child returned with a small necklace in her hand. It had a cross on it, and engraved on the cross was an inscription saying that all things were possible with God's help.

"Here, take this." She stepped onto the chair and fastened the necklace around Karina's neck. "I'm not going to let you give up. You are going to fly again. Someday, so am I."

Karina choked back tears. "I'll think about it. Thanks." She hugged Penny tightly, slipped a nightgown onto the child, and took her downstairs for ice cream and a "short" game of Monopoly.

Later, listening to Penny's peaceful slumber, Karina thought about the brave girl cuddled beside her. If only she could be as brave, she would not only be flying, but would have conquered the fears and nightmares that relentlessly tormented her.

After reflecting on the tragic events that had brought Penny into her life, and hours of soul-searching, Karina had an idea, a wild idea. Still, she might be able to pull it off if she was brave enough, if she appealed to Martin's sense of justice. She made a mental note to discuss her idea with him the very next day, or, as the clock indicated, this very day.

* * *

After breakfast, Karina asked Mrs. Winfield to drive her to the airport where she knew Martin would be working on some aspect of the trip. She then requested, and was granted, a meeting with him. He said he had wanted to speak with her anyhow, but he certainly wasn't ready for the discussion at hand.

"Are you serious?" Martin asked, sitting up in amazement. He peered across a paper-cluttered desk into her eyes. Karina met his gaze without wavering.

"Yes, sir, very serious," she said. "I can do it. I know I can." Her hand went instinctively to the cross hanging around her neck.

"Karina," Martin said, not unpleasantly, "you are grounded because you disobeyed a command, a command given to help ensure your safety and the safety of your fellow classmates. You ignored that command and jeopardized your safety and their safety. Until we resolve that issue, you will remain grounded. Even then, there is no way that I am going to allow you to take anyone up alone. Do you understand?"

Karina nodded, tried to think up a response, but Martin continued after a short pause.

"You do seem to have made progress though, so you can forget the early curfew."

She lowered her head to hide her frustration and tears, her confidence slipping. This was not the way she had rehearsed the conversation. "I understand. Sorry." She turned to leave the room before Martin could see her cry.

"Karina," Martin said. "If you want Penny to have a flight, I'd be delighted to take her as soon as the weather breaks."

Karina couldn't respond. The tears were streaming from her eyes. Without turning back, she simply shook her head and left before anything else could go wrong. All day, she dodged Martin, her friends, and classmates. She did her chores silently and asked Sally to take her home. Home. Yes, that's how she felt about the Winfields. They were family.

All evening, she was quiet. Even Mrs. Winfield and Penny couldn't remove the gloom from her face. She begged off on playing checkers and watching television, saying she had a headache and wanted to get some rest.

Mrs. Winfield suggested she go on to bed and Penny would sleep in her own room, which brought about an immediate argument between mother and daughter, but Karina left before its conclusion.

After undressing and slipping into bed, the flood gave way. She cried for a long time, and then slept. She would have slept all night, except for the nightmare, her first since coming to the Winfields' home. She woke trembling, heart pounding in her ears.

The patter of little feet caught her attention. Quietly, a small figure dressed in T-shirt and panties flipped on the lights and hopped into bed next to her.

"Karina?" asked Penny anxiously. "What's wrong? What's happened?"

Karina rolled over, her hands cold and clammy. She forced a weak smile for the little girl.

"Sorry. Just a nightmare. Did I wake you?"

Penny nodded, "I heard you all the way down the hall. Was it bad?" She snuggled up to Karina.

"Yes, but it's better now. I just had a bad day. My nightmares come when I'm either frightened or upset about something."

"What's bothering you? You've been acting strange all day." Penny patted Karina's arm. "Can I help?"

"No," she said. "I'm okay now."

Penny kept up a dialog, wheedling out what had caused Karina's nightmare this time. She wouldn't stop no matter what; she wouldn't leave even if Karina called her mom, which she informed Karina would lead to a spanking because she wasn't supposed to be out of her room until morning for any reason. She was being punished for arguing about sleeping with Karina.

Penny got so loud and demanding that Karina gave in to keep the little girl out of trouble. She thought of lying, but decided against it.

"I tried to get my teacher to let me fly again. I wanted to take you up in one of our two-seat planes, but he said no," Karina said. "I'm still being punished." She didn't add that Martin felt she might not be safe to ride with. She didn't want to break Penny's image of her.

Penny thought for long seconds. "Have you tried bargaining?"

"What do you mean, bargaining?" She looked into Penny's sky blue eyes.

"Well, sometimes, when I'm in big trouble and receive a long punishment, like being grounded from television for a week, I bargain my way out. I exchange one punishment for another. Last time, I exchanged taking out the garbage and doing dishes every night for two weeks in place of not using the telephone for a week."

"I'm not sure this is in the same category," Karina said, but the idea was intriguing. Maybe Martin would be willing to change her punishment, if she showed him she was sincere, if she picked something harsh enough to be serious. Maybe he would let her fly again, and if he did, maybe she could convince him to let her take Penny up. By the time Penny departed for her own room and sleep overtook Karina, she had developed a plan that just might impress on Martin how serious she was about flying, and about helping fulfill Penny's dream.

* * *

Karina entered the tiny room and found Martin seated at a small wooden desk grading the previous day's geography tests and listening to the weather radio, which stated that the rain was letting up. The forecast was for two or three days of clearing before a new weather system hit the Gulf Coast, possibly bringing another long period of rain.

"Sir, may I speak with you for a minute?" Karina stood in front of Martin's makeshift desk, hands clasped in front of her.

"Sure, Karina." Martin gestured for her to sit. "What is it?"

"I want to fly. I need to fly." She scrutinized Martin's every expression.

"I thought we've been all through that," Martin said.

"Sir, I'd like to bargain for a new punishment, anything so I can fly." Karina remembered Penny's advice. "I really need to fly."

"Please, sit." Martin again motioned her to a chair. Ignoring the previous day's conversation, he said, "What do you have in mind, Karina, and why is flying suddenly so important? Just a few days ago, you swore you were never going to get into another plane."

She remained standing. "As far as flying, I was trying to run away from something I should have dealt with years ago. I know that now. Some things just can't be ignored."

While she spoke, Karina discovered the truth in her words. She had learned from a seriously ill, courageous, eleven-year-old girl that life was what she made it. No sense crying about what couldn't be changed. Stand tall and live each day as it came.

"About my punishment," she said. "I need it changed to deal with my fear, to discover who I really am. I need it for me." Karina ended with Penny's very words from the night before, not because they sounded impressive but because they were true.

Martin sat silently, waiting for her to continue. His expression gave Karina no indication whether or not he was impressed by her announcement. She certainly had a lot to overcome. How many times had she stood before him, defiant, selfishly seeking her own way? Could Martin possibly see that she was serious? That she had changed? That she was not the same girl he had grounded just days earlier? Could she appeal to his instincts and gain a closer evaluation?

"I would like to trade being grounded for a spanking," Karina spoke slowly, clearly. Through borrowed courage, she maintained eye contact with the person whose decision directed her future.

Martin's expression changed little, but she had his full attention. It had taken her a long time to think up a punishment that showed she was serious, still allowed her freedom to be with Penny, and could, perhaps, help regain flying privileges. Actually, the punishment was Penny's unknown suggestion. Karina had been impressed with the child's willingness to face such a consequence to comfort her after the terrible nightmare. Could she do less in return?

"Wow," Martin ended the awkward silence that greeted her announcement. "That's quite a sacrifice. Don't you have any other alternatives?"

She couldn't tell if Martin was serious or just testing her resolve. Either way, she had made her decision and would live with it.

"No, sir. Can we get it over with, please?" she asked, hoping that a quick response would sway Martin into agreement.

"All right, your flight status is reinstated as soon as weather permits." Martin sighed. "But before you even think about flying alone, you're going prove to me that you can handle flying under any situation. Agreed?"

She nodded. This was going much better than expected. She almost repeated her request to take Penny up before they left Fulton but thought better of it—no sense in pushing too far.

To Karina's amazement, Martin's attention turned to grading papers. Had he forgotten about the spanking? She thought about saying nothing, leaving before he remembered, but that would mean running away again. She was better than that, or at least she hoped she was.

"Sir, what about my punishment?" she asked.

Martin put down his marking pen and sat back in his chair. He started to say something, but then changed his mind, shaking his head. Once again, he motioned for her to sit. This time, she accepted.

"You really are serious, aren't you?" he asked. Then, before she could speak, "What does discipline mean to you, Karina?"

"Well." She groped for words. "It means to be punished for something you've done wrong."

"True," Martin said. "But what is the objective, the goal of good discipline?"

Her response took longer this time. "To keep you from doing something wrong, something bad?"

Martin nodded. "That's part of it. When I grounded you, it was to keep you from making a mistake and hurting yourself or someone else. Later, I said you would remain grounded until the issue was resolved. In my opinion, it has now been resolved.

"A punishment should fit the crime," he said. "You disobeyed because you were not fully in control of yourself. Your emotions were controlling your actions, putting yourself and others in danger. Now, I believe, you have faced the problem, and the only way we will know for sure is to put you back into the air.

"As far as spanking you, I don't see a need. Such punishment is only effective when a child uses poor judgment and deliberately disobeys. For that to happen, the child must be in control. You were not in control; therefore, spanking you would solve nothing and might even make matters worse. The discipline would become the focus, and not your actions.

"Secondly, now that you've come to understand the real problem, I don't believe any punishment is necessary. Your willingness to accept severe punishment indicates your readiness to deal with the cause of your disobedience. I can't expect more."

Karina saw the wisdom in Martin's reasoning. She was ready, not totally sure what the outcome would be, but willing, even eager, to begin.

"I sent you to the Winfields so you could learn to look outside yourself, something we've had limited success with," Martin said. "I had a hunch Penny might rub off on you. She's such a special child. Her father and I have been friends since college."

"It worked," Karina said. "I feel at home there, and I truly love Penny. I don't think I could handle what she's going through. Is she getting better?"

"Her disease is in remission now, and has been for about a year," Martin said. "She has not always responded to treatment. Penny needs a bone marrow transplant, but a suitable donor hasn't been found. Her blood type is quite rare."

"What about her parents? Shouldn't one of them have the same blood type?" Karina asked. She had a vague recollection from a science class that blood types were handed down genetically.

"Penny has the same blood type as her natural father." Martin said. "Unfortunately, it is not a common type."

Karina was stunned. "Natural father? Dr. Winfield isn't Penny's father?"

"No, she's adopted," Martin said. "Her natural father died from leukemia while Penny was still a baby, and her mother died of breast cancer when she was three. Cancer seems to be genetically prevalent in her natural family. Penny contracted leukemia at age seven."

Now was as good a time as any, Karina thought. She took the plunge. "I have to take Penny up. She needs to fly, for herself and no one else. It's not just the plane ride; it's her life's dream, and I'm part of it now."

"So, that's it," Martin said. "I won't say no; I won't say yes. I'm not sure you're capable of carrying out what you're asking, so let's leave it at maybe, and take it from there when the weather clears. Now, get out of here before I spank you for keeping me from finishing here."

"Right," Karina said. She felt like she could fly, airplane or no airplane.

That evening, after informing Penny of her reinstated flight status, Karina spent hours teaching the little bundle of energy everything she knew about flying ultralights, every story, every detail. Only a mother's wisdom got them to bed at a respectable hour, and then, only with an unstated threat hidden within Mrs. Winfield's gentle commands.

Next morning dawned bright and clear, and Martin was true to his words. He had Karina in the air shortly after breakfast. They were in *Jet Stream*, Karina in back and Martin in the front seat.

Hour after hour, Karina performed every maneuver Martin threw at her: tight spins, turns, stalls, everything. She made some mistakes, but not big ones. Even when Martin suddenly took control and put them in a steep, spinning dive, Karina didn't panic. Her heart pounded, but she didn't panic.

When she thought she had done everything possible, Martin ordered her to climb to 12,000-feet, as high as a small plane was supposed to fly without the aid of oxygen. At first, she wasn't sure she had heard him right. She made him repeat the command three times before ascending. The ground pulled away. Trees became a carpet of grass, and houses looked smaller than match sticks.

Martin explained that during the third phase of the journey, they would fly over mountains. He had adjusted the fuel rate to compensate for that altitude and wanted to see how the plane performed.

During those days, Penny was a permanent fixture around the airport. When Karina wasn't flying, they were always together. Penny turned out to be a fast learner and soaked up information like a sponge. It was a happy time for both girls.

Then, it was over. A hurricane in the Gulf of Mexico changed course, giving them a window of opportunity to begin the next phase of the journey. They were headed south to the Lake of the Ozarks. There, they would install amphibious floats onto the ultralights and practice landing on water.

Farther west, especially near the mountains, landing sites would be more difficult to find. Adding the amphibious floats would give them a chance to land on any lake more than 200-yards across.

Karina tried several times to get Martin to let her take Penny for a ride, but he firmly denied her requests. Once she pushed too far, was too demanding, too impertinent, and got smacked on the seat for her effort, with a further warning to get out before she lost her flight status again.

Penny hugged her tightly on that final morning, not wanting Karina to leave. It was the first time she had seen the little girl cry. Karina put her in *Meadow Lark* until the last minute, and then they were gone.

Flying away from her newly adopted family was the hardest thing Karina had done since leaving her homeland. She cried quietly to herself. Once again she was flying third in formation, just ahead of Joe and Martin. She didn't try to conceal her misery from the others, for they too had become attached to Fulton and its hospitality. It wasn't until they sighted the twisting, expansive fingers of water that made up the Lake of the Ozarks that their attention was diverted from past to present.

Chapter 9

Water Landings and Dreams Fulfilled

Warm sunshine rose in the east and highlighted the sparkling blue lake outside Martin's cabin. Already, Karina and her companions had been sitting attentively around the polished oak table in Martin's cabin for over an hour. Two days had come and gone since leaving Fulton. During that time, they had landed at a small airport near Lake of the Ozarks, Missouri, settled into resort cabins, and gone to work installing amphibious floats onto the ultralights. A day and a half was necessary for removing the wheels, uncrating parts, taking inventory, making sense out of the directions, and attaching the odd-shaped amphibious floats. Then, they were subjected to endless lectures on the physics and procedures for landing and taking off on water.

"Remember." Martin drummed his fingers on the table for emphasis. "Flight dynamics for takeoff on water are the same as on land. You must have proper airspeed before you begin climbing. It'll take you longer to reach minimum airspeed, so don't worry about distance. It's a big lake; use it."

"Sir, what about boats?" Joe asked. "The lake has a lot of traffic on it."

"Early mornings, most are filled with fishermen anchored near the shore fishing for crappie," Martin explained between gulps of hot black coffee. "We should be fine as long as we stay in the main channel. The real danger will be after ten o'clock in the morning when speedboats and skiers take to the lake. That's why we woke you so early. We must finish this morning by nine-thirty."

Karina surveyed her fellow pilots and wondered if they were as tired as she was. Paul followed every word Martin said, but he had his head propped up with both hands, elbows balanced on the table. Joe leaned back in his chair half asleep, and why not? It was his day off. His only job for the day was to videotape their performance. Jessica and Megan fidgeted nervously and shifted in their seats throughout the lecture.

"If there are no other questions, let's hit it." Martin grabbed his helmet and headed for the door.

Twenty minutes later found the group lakeside in a remote cove. A light fog lingered over the water, slowly dissipating in the sun's early morning warmth. Martin and Sally had landed the newly-altered ultralights just before sunset the day before and tied them to a float dock normally reserved for boats. It took quite a bit of paperwork and planning before Martin had acquired authorization to land on the lake.

On this historic morning, the ground crew had the planes fully fueled and inspected, so the pilots only had to do a normal preflight. Within 10 short minutes, all six planes were occupied. Karina flew second today, just behind Sally. Paul, Megan, and Jessica followed. As usual, Martin brought up the rear. Each pilot would make two takeoffs and landings. If all went well, they would be done in a little over an hour. Then, after debriefing, they were free to enjoy the shopping mall, the carnival rides that lined each side of the main highway, sightseeing or whatever pleased them.

Karina applied steady pressure to her throttle and followed Sally away from the dock. On water, the plane functioned similar to a boat. In fact, Karina felt like she was driving a boat. Each pilot wore a life jacket, just in case—nobody had asked in case of what.

She adjusted her speed to maintain a safe distance behind Sally. The rising sun swept away the last hint of fog and provided good visibility. They were lucky. The fog could have remained much longer, which often happened early in the morning when air temperature and water temperature varied by more than a few degrees.

Karina keyed her microphone. "*Lady Bird* requesting permission to position for takeoff. Over." She wished she was flying *Meadow Lark*, but it wasn't her turn. Sally passed by on her takeoff run.

"Permission granted, make your turn. Over," Martin answered.

Karina made a counterclockwise turn, careful not to overcorrect with the rudder. The plane responded well, and she was in position for takeoff. Unlike the small fields and runways they used on land, the lake seemed to stretch ahead for miles. *This should be no problem*, she thought grasping the cross around her neck. She missed Penny terribly.

"Ground control to *Lady Bird*. Over," Joe called.

"*Lady Bird*. Over," Karina said. It was nice to be with Joe again. She hadn't seen much of him while she was living with the Winfields.

"Wind is from the west at ten knots. Watch the windsock on the flotation buoy. Sally reported a sudden gust on her takeoff. Good luck, Rini. Over," Joe said, using his new nickname for her.

Karina knew that Joe really liked her and wanted to be her "steady," but each time he tried to develop a closer relationship, something got in the way.

"Roger. Wind from the west at ten knots and watch the windsock," she repeated. "Thanks, Joe. I'll be careful. Over."

Karina shoved the throttle fully forward and glanced at the windsock. Her plane lunged ahead, and the floats sliced effortlessly through the calm lake water. Martin's warning proved correct. She ate up a lot more distance than she expected. However, her airspeed inched upward: 30, 35, 40, 45, 50, 55.

She pulled the control stick toward her. The plane shuttered a little and lifted from the water. At first, Karina flew just above the lake's surface, not trying to climb. She had plenty of lake before her and wanted more airspeed before leaving ground effect for higher altitude.

At 60-miles per hour, Karina increased pressure on her control stick and climbed to pattern altitude, 2000-feet. Below her, the scenery was breathtaking. Blue water, surrounded by lush green rolling hills, stretched for as far as the eye could see. Karina wished she had Penny with her. The kid would go crazy. Karina vowed to come back here somehow and fulfill her friend's dream. When and how, she wasn't sure, but someday.

Karina had little time for reminiscing. She had already circled the bright blue finger of lake they used for their runway. She noticed Martin rising from the water in *Jet Stream*.

"Continue circling and watch my lead," Sally radioed the airborne pilots. "Check your spacing and keep an eye out for other light aircraft. We're not the only ones up here. Small aircraft and helicopters tour this area on sightseeing excursions. Remember, they aren't using our frequency, so stay sharp. Over."

Everyone performed as directed. Two circles around the lake, and all six planes were airborne in tight formation. Lining up for landing proved even easier—keep the plane centered on the middle of the lake and descend normally.

Karina enjoyed the experience and wanted to keep at it for a while longer, but as usual, Martin was correct. Boats were moving from docks and little coves into the main channel. Remaining in the air much longer might make landing tricky and cause some poor fisherman heart failure. She doubted that flying fish were on the menu.

Karina lined up for landing and followed Sally down. Landing was a breeze, and Joe met her when she pulled up to the dock. He smiled and walked strangely, like he was hiding something behind his back. Other ground team members secured the planes.

"Hey," he shouted, as she killed her engine and popped open the canopy window. "You in the mood for surprises?"

"Always, if they're good," she said. Karina logged her flight in her logbook and hopped out while Valerie tied *Lady Bird* to the dock. Karina faced Joe and tried to see what he was hiding behind his back, but he moved away, forcing her to come toward him.

"What's the surprise?" she shouted above an ultralight engine. Megan pulled up to the dock.

"Close your eyes," Joe said. "Don't cheat."

"I'm not a cheater." Karina closed her eyes and placed her hands behind her back. She dreamed about Joe crossing over and kissing her, but she couldn't believe he'd do it in front of everyone. Martin would go ballistic.

Seconds later, two arms circled her waist and clung tightly to her. Karina opened her eyes to the most wonderful sight, a little blond head pressed tightly against her. Karina lifted Penny and returned the hug a hundredfold.

"What are you doing here?" she said in a stern mother-like tone. "You didn't run away from home did you?" Karina was half teasing, half serious, and completely happy.

"Daddy brought us," Penny said. "I was so moody the last couple of days that he decided the whole family needed to get away for a short vacation. He gave me a choice of where to go, and where else would I choose?"

"Where, indeed?" Karina hugged her again. "How long can you stay?"

"Five days," said Penny. "Until after the Fourth of July."

"Hey, that's strange." Karina tousled Penny's hair. "That's exactly how long we're going to be here. Imagine that!"

Feeling left out, Joe joined them. He took Karina's flight helmet and helped her out of her flight suit. They finished tying down the planes, and Penny said hello to the rest of her newfound friends before everyone headed for the vans. Martin was just pulling up to the dock.

"Karina, you fly great!" Penny said wistfully as the girls walked up the steps. "I hope I can do as well someday."

"Hey, you think that's something," Joe said. "Wait until tomorrow when you can see a real pilot at work."

"That's right," Karina said. "Keep your eyes on *Meadow Lark* tomorrow."

"I'm not flying *Meadow Lark* tomorrow," said Joe. They topped the long wooden stairs and reached the vans.

"I know," Karina replied smugly. "I am."

Joe chased her around the parking area, dodging around and between the school's long 15-passenger vans, while Penny, Dr. and Mrs. Winfield, and an assortment of the ground crew laughed at their childishness. Joe would have caught Karina, but Martin reached the top of the stairs and interceded. It took only a quick reminder that the day was free after debriefing to interrupt the shenanigans and get everyone headed back to the cabins.

Debriefing went quickly. Martin was pleased with everyone's performance and simply informed them to remember their ten o'clock curfew and that they were not to go anywhere alone. He was available to drive them around town. All they had to do was ask.

Karina and Joe went with the Winfields. Dr. Winfield treated them to lunch, then drove them to the Outlet Mall, the biggest shopping center Karina had ever seen, more than a hundred stores scattered over acres.

"Here." Dr. Winfield shoved a thick envelope into Karina's hand. "You kids have a good time. I promised my wife we'd do some shopping in peace. You don't mind if Penny tags along, do you?"

"Of course not." Karina squeezed Penny's hand and opened the envelope. It had $150 inside. Karina threw her arms around Dr. Winfield, hugged him, then tried to give back the money. "Thank you, but I can't take this. It's too much."

"Keep it. I insist. You're part of our family now, Karina. Besides, I never paid you for sitting with Penny. Your companionship has meant a lot to her. Buy something for yourself and enjoy. We'll pick you up here for dinner at five o'clock. No arguments and don't be late."

The rest of the day was a dream come true. They wandered from one specialty outlet store to another. Karina bought some new shorts, a pair of jeans, two tops, and some jewelry. She also shared her wealth, buying Joe a new sports watch and Penny some pierced earrings.

Dinner was at an exclusive seafood restaurant, followed by an exciting evening of carnival rides, miniature golf, midget car races, and ice cream. Joe alternately held hands with Karina and Penny. They enjoyed one activity after another. Karina couldn't remember the last time she'd had such fun. Not since she lost her parents had she been this happy.

All too soon, Dr. Winfield informed them curfew was fast approaching. Penny started to beg for more time, but her father's warning look instantly squelched any resistance. Still, it had been a wonderful day, and Karina had to admit that she was tired. Tomorrow morning would be another five o'clock start.

Martin waited for them at the resort's entrance. He thanked Dr. Winfield for watching them and making sure they were back on time.

While he talked with the Winfields, Karina hugged Penny good night. The excitement had done what Karina wouldn't have believed possible. The little girl was worn out, and crawled into the back of the station wagon. Karina tucked her under a blanket on the back seat, and Penny was asleep almost before Karina kissed her good night.

Joe waited until Karina emerged from the car, then pulled her around the corner of the building out of Martin's and the Winfields' sight. He hugged Karina to him and kissed her. He put her hands in his and inserted something small into them, his old school ring.

"Please wear this. I love you." That was all he said.

Before Karina could catch her breath and kiss Joe back, he was gone. Martin approached before she could call after Joe, and Karina heard the Winfields' car pulling away. Martin stopped beside her and put a hand on her shoulder.

"Karina, you did very well today," he said seriously. "You really seemed to be enjoying yourself this morning. Keep it up tomorrow and the next day. Then, come and see me."

Karina waited for Martin to say more, but he seemed lost in thought, staring past her at something Karina could not see. She squeezed the ring tighter. Had he seen Joe kiss her or pass her the ring? She knew intimate contact was forbidden at Blue Horizons. It could get one of them transferred to another program, but Martin's praise didn't fit the scenario she was building.

Martin patted her on the shoulder, told her to get some rest, and headed toward his own room in the cabin nearest the lake. He stopped at each cabin along the way to ensure everyone obeyed curfew.

Karina slipped into the cabin she shared with Jessica, Megan, and Valerie. The others were already asleep. She quickly undressed, showered, and crawled into bed, but Martin's conversation droned in her head, and it was hours later before she found sleep.

During the next two days, Karina strived to impress Martin. Her concentration during practice and demonstration flights had never been better. She was comfortable with water landings, and out of all the students, only Joe's flying ability topped hers. Karina wanted every maneuver to be perfect. In a way, she was showing off for Penny, who dragged her parents out of bed every morning before daylight to make sure she was at the lake in time for Karina's takeoff.

The weather remained perfect. For the time being, the expected storms in the Gulf of Mexico had stalled out in the Atlantic, but Martin insisted that bad weather was on the way. He said it was going to be a long wet summer because the water of the Atlantic was already so warm. Martin explained that warm ocean water caused hurricanes, and the group decided they were glad they weren't closer to the unsettled ocean area.

Because of boat traffic on the lake, only early morning flights were possible. Lessons were suspended, except for one 2-hour period ending just before lunch. The afternoons and evenings, until curfew, were free. This gave the kids plenty of time for sightseeing, shopping, swimming, and just hanging out.

Karina spent free time with the Winfields, which seemed to suit Martin just fine. Joe became a permanent fixture. Dr. Winfield joked that he always wanted a son, but somehow thought he'd start with a somewhat younger child.

July 3rd excited everyone with the promise of a day and a half off and a huge fireworks display scheduled to begin at dusk on July 4th. The kids wouldn't fly that day. Martin was giving them a holiday, a day of rest. Their flight across the nation would resume early on July 5th.

As instructed two days earlier, Karina knocked on Martin's door shortly before curfew. She had finished another wonderful day, and the Winfields had just dropped her off. She was nervous about responding to this request. Her flying had been excellent, and she knew Martin was pleased, so there should be no reason for anxiety. Still, she couldn't push the strangeness of Martin's request from her mind. The way he had looked into space still haunted her. Something was up. She just wasn't sure what it was. Could this be some kind of a trap? Was something unexpected sneaking up on her, something waiting to catch her off guard?

"Come in. It's open," Martin called in answer to her knock.

Karina entered and found her instructor leaning over a small table covered with aerial maps. He didn't look up as she entered, so she stood quietly waiting for him to finish, to acknowledge her presence.

"Have a seat." Martin waved in the general direction of the large brown sofa lining one living room wall. "I'll be finished in a moment. We're waiting for Sally. She should be here any minute now."

Karina sat down. Martin's cabin was smaller than the kids' cabins, probably because he had it all to himself, whereas the kids were stuck four to a cabin. He had placed dozens of aerial photos on two easel-supported bulletin boards. Red circles marked several places on each photo. Some had as many as four circles. Karina saw that each circle surrounded a clear area, maybe landing sites.

Sally entered with a six-pack of cold soda and a large pepperoni pizza, handed a Coke to Karina, placed the pizza on the countertop and sat beside her on the sofa. Martin finished whatever he was doing and sat in a wicker chair across from them. Suspense filled the room, making Karina nervous. Her stomach filled with butterflies, and she placed her soda on the coffee table in front of her.

"Karina," Martin said slowly, as if carefully choosing his words. "I've got some good news for you, and some not so good news. Which do you want to hear first?"

Karina's heart jumped. What bad news could there be? Was Martin upset with her developing relationship with Joe? Had the court decided for her to return home? Her mind jumped from one possibility to another.

"The bad news," she whispered, her words as shaky as her quaking stomach.

"I thought so." Martin crossed the room, knelt beside Karina, and in an extraordinary gesture, took her hands in his.

Sally moved closer. Karina felt panic. Whatever the news, they expected it to have a dramatic effect on her.

Martin looked straight into Karina's eyes. "Dr. Winfield informed me, when they joined us a couple of days ago, that Penny's latest blood test was not good. Her disease is active again. They haven't told Penny yet, but a bone marrow transplant must be performed shortly if she is to survive."

Karina gasped, the air driven from her as if a huge fist had slammed into her tormented lungs. The room revolved around her, growing darker.

* * *

"You're okay. Just relax." Sally's soothing voice reached through the fog. "Don't move yet. Lie still."

She was lying on the sofa, legs propped up on several pillows, a position Karina recognized as the classic shock prevention method. She started to speak, but Martin cut her off before she found her voice.

"Sorry. I know that was a terrible shock. At first, I wasn't going to tell you, but I decided that not telling you wouldn't be fair. You've worked so hard at dealing with your own loss that I decided you could handle this," he said, maintaining continuous eye contact, watching her for any further signs of distress. "Besides, if I hadn't told you, you would have been suspicious about the good news I have for you."

With Sally's gentle help guiding her, Karina sat up. Tears ran down her face as if they had a life of their own. Outwardly, she wasn't crying, but the tears kept coming anyway. It was annoying. Inwardly, she had known something was wrong with Penny. The kid needed frequent rest periods and was always ready for bed at night, something uncommon during Karina's stay with the Winfields.

"What good news?" She wiped tears away with her sleeve until Martin fetched tissues from the bathroom.

"Tomorrow, you're going to fly Sally to Spirit of St. Louis Airport, a mid-sized tower-controlled airport about twenty miles from downtown St. Louis." He handed her the tissues. "After a short break, you'll refuel and fly back here. You'll have to be careful. This trip will push the ultralight's range; however, it's still within the safety margin."

Any other time this challenge and responsibility would have been fantastic news indeed. Now, however, it seemed like punishment. She had promised Penny they would spend the day together, and with what Martin had just told her, she wanted to keep that promise more than ever.

"How is that good news?" she asked, fingers nervously crushing the damp tissues. "I promised Penny we'd spend the day together. I don't want to leave her. I want to spend as much time with her as possible."

Martin held up his hands for silence. "You will leave at first light, land at Fulton where Joe and I will be waiting to top off your fuel tank, and fly straight to Spirit. You should be back here no later than one o'clock in the afternoon. That will give you the rest of the day with Penny. Her parents are going to let her sleep late tomorrow. They've told her that she must be rested, or she'll have to take a lengthy nap in the afternoon. They've also informed her that you have a special class tomorrow, which in a way you do."

"I'd still..." Karina began, but Martin's expression generated silence.

"That's not all," he said. "The good news is that a donor has been found for Penny, and a bone marrow transplant is scheduled for the morning of the sixth. Therefore, someone must deliver Penny to St. Louis on the fifth. Want the job?"

Comprehension penetrated slowly through cascading emotions, first suppressing, then uplifting her spirits. Karina didn't dare believe what Martin had just implied. He was not known for breaking with procedure. She'd asked only to take Penny for a quick circle around the area, a request unceremoniously denied. A cross-country flight was in dreamland.

"You mean I can fly Penny to St. Louis?" Her volume was so low, she wondered if she had spoken at all.

"That's exactly what I mean," said Martin. "If you're up to it, and tomorrow's flight proves you capable. Penny needs to be in good spirits when she reaches St. Louis. Your fulfilling her dream and being near during the procedure would be a tremendous help."

"I'll fly the lead plane. You'll follow me all the way, no silliness," he said. "Dr. and Mrs. Winfield will be at Spirit to chauffeur us to the hospital. An adjoining hospital room has been provided for you and Mrs. Winfield. I'll check into a nearby hotel."

The shock of Penny's condition and Martin's incredible offer drained Karina. She wasn't sure she was thinking straight, but she was extremely grateful for Martin's concern and the opportunity to fly Penny to St. Louis. He had earned a friend for life.

An hour later, after a careful study of the aerial maps and territory between Lake of the Ozarks and St. Louis, Karina showered and bedded down in Sally's cabin. Martin wanted her fresh and rested. He also wanted to keep the other kids from finding out about the flight until it was under way. He didn't want any slip of the tongue to raise Penny's suspicion.

* * *

"Spirit tower, this is Alpha November three—five—seven. We're five miles out, requesting permission to enter the pattern." Karina used the official numbers on *Jet Stream*. Their common name wasn't important to a control tower. The two-seat ultralights were Federal Aviation Rule 103 exempt trainers, which meant they were not true ultralights but were exempted under special FAA regulations. When landing at larger controlled towers, however, formal procedure had to be followed.

Karina received permission to enter the landing pattern. The control tower instructed her to land third, behind two much larger commuter airplanes. She landed without incident, and Sally directed her to a parking area.

They ate a quick lunch at the cafeteria, refueled, and headed toward Fulton. A cloudless sky, little head wind, and cruising at 70-miles per hour rapidly chewed up distance. Karina willed the little plane ahead. She seldom spoke during the flight. Sally seemed to understand and left Karina to herself as much as possible.

Shortly past noon, they landed at Fulton, where Martin and Joe waited with gas for the final hop. Sally and Martin fueled the ultralight, while Joe pulled Karina aside.

"What's this all about?" Joe asked. "Martin wouldn't tell me a thing. He gave me some yarn about making sure you were ready to fly west, but everyone knows how well you're flying lately. There aren't any storms in the area, so it's all a mystery. What's up?"

Karina sipped from a tall glass of ice-cold lemonade Martin had provided. "Joe, I can't tell you now. I promised. Tomorrow you'll know everything."

She badly wanted to confide in him, but she had given her word. Martin was graciously allowing her to fulfill Penny's dream. She would honor his request, no matter what. Joe was put out, but for now, there was nothing Karina could do about it. She quickly downed the rest of her lemonade, hurried to the bathroom and returned to work.

Refueling completed, Karina wasted no time winging her way to Lake of the Ozarks. The entire round-trip took a little under eight hours. She found Penny sitting on the boat dock, waiting impatiently for her return.

"What took so long?" she asked in a whiny voice as soon as Karina opened the canopy window. "I've been waiting for hours. How far did you go?"

Karina lifted Penny off her feet, hugged her, and steered her toward the cabins. Karina wanted to change out of her flight suit and shower. Martin and Joe were driving back, and she wanted to be ready to go into town the moment they returned.

Penny was filthy from fooling around in the mud at the edge of the lake while she awaited their return, so Karina made her shower as well. The little girl kept up a steady stream of chatter until finally Karina playfully shoved her face under the showerhead, which led to a short water fight that Karina let Penny win.

By the time Martin and Joe returned from Fulton, both girls were ready for an afternoon on the town. Once more, Dr. and Mrs. Winfield treated them to dinner and a great time. The best fireworks display Karina had ever seen capped off the evening. The only drawback the entire day was Penny's fatigue. Twice during the day, she fell asleep while Dr. Winfield drove them from one event to another. The fatigue brought with it the stark reality of Penny's life-threatening illness.

At the resort that evening, Martin greeted the group and informed Penny that Karina was going to take her on a long plane ride tomorrow. The little girl's eyes lit up, and she beamed with joy, her fatigue quickly forgotten.

"That's why you were gone so long today!" Penny shouted, bouncing up and down with each word. "You were practicing for me." She hugged Karina tightly.

Karina saw Joe's mouth fall open in amazement with the announcement. She knew he was having difficulty believing his ears. A student flying anyone other than an instructor was simply impossible. If Martin hadn't been the one to announce the coming event, Joe probably would have thought it a lie.

"Karina, what's this about?" he asked after Penny was carried away by her parents with the stern warning that she depart for bed immediately or she would travel by car tomorrow instead.

Karina looked to Martin, who nodded approval. "I'm flying Penny to St. Louis for a bone marrow operation that we hope may save her life. Her leukemia is active again. The hospital has found a compatible donor. It's kind of like a last chance for her."

Karina's voice quavered, and Joe gave her a brief reassuring hug. He didn't seem to know exactly what to say but appeared determined to lend any support possible. Martin seemed to understand Joe's intention and ignored the intimate contact.

Joe finally found words to speak. "Hey, everything will turn out fine. I heard that this type of operation is becoming routine. Penny's a fighter. She'll come through it. Wait and see."

Karina lifted her head from Joe's shoulder and stared into the soft kindness of his sparkling eyes. "I know she's a fighter, but she's so little. She reminds me more of a five-year-old sometimes, and fighting for life is a very grown-up battle."

"She's not fighting alone. You'll be with her, and the rest of us will be praying and pulling for her every minute. You give her the time of her life tomorrow, and she'll be back, pestering for more rides in no time. We'll have to fly west just to get some peace and quiet."

Karina laughed weakly, grateful for Joe's humor and perspective. He was correct about one thing. Penny would not be fighting alone.

Martin let them sit and talk for almost an hour before gently reminding Karina that she needed to be sharp tomorrow. Good nights were exchanged and everyone drifted away, each lost in his or her own thoughts.

Morning dawned clear, and Karina marveled at the golden sunrise inching its way into a brilliant blue, cloudless sky. It would be a good day for flying. Preflight had gone without a hitch, and now she sat on the grass next to her plane, enjoying the coming day, and anxiously awaiting Penny's arrival.

Martin and Sally conversed quietly next to the hangar. The cool morning air produced a light ground fog just above the warm earth. The effect was stunning, carpeting the entire area, and giving one the sensation of walking through clouds.

Karina wondered if heaven looked like this, angels walking among the clouds, no fears or worries to disturb the peace and serenity of the moment. The thought brought her back to Penny, and she pondered what the future held for her tiny friend. How would Penny react when they arrived and her parents broke the news? Talk about a letdown; going from the fulfillment of one's greatest dream to death's doorstep. Death. Just the thought of it made her shudder. Well, there was nothing she could do to protect Penny, so Karina was determined to make this flight something very special.

The Winfields' station wagon pulled around the corner, and it was time to begin. Karina got to her feet and cheerfully greeted Penny, who bounced out of the car almost before it came to a complete stop. She raced to Karina.

"Hi, kid. Are you ready to fly?"

"You bet!" Penny grabbed Karina's hands and jumped up and down, her blonde hair flying in all directions.

"Hey, take it easy. We've got a long flight ahead of us. I don't want you napping and missing the view."

"Oh, I wouldn't," Penny said. "This is going to be the best day of my life. I don't want to miss a minute."

At Penny's words, tears welled up in Karina's eyes, and she quickly turned away using the sleeve of her flight suit for a handkerchief.

Dr. Winfield came to the rescue. He picked up his daughter, giving her a firm hug. "You listen to Karina and Martin. Mom and I will meet you shortly after you land. We drive almost as fast as you fly, so the wait shouldn't be too long." He placed Penny on the ground.

"I'll do everything Karina and Martin say," Penny said. "If we fly close enough to the road, wave to me."

"Mom and I will be looking for you." He turned to Karina. "Take good care of my girl for me. Thanks for everything."

Before Karina could respond, Dr. Winfield walked to Martin and Sally, spoke a few words, and left to pick his wife up for the drive to St. Louis.

"Karina, get Penny into a flight suit and go over how to use the intercom," Martin said, his way of formal greeting. "We need to get moving."

She marched the child to *Jet Stream* and pulled out a flight suit specially made for Penny. Sally had worked diligently all night on it.

"For me?" asked Penny, her eyes wide with surprise. "It's beautiful."

Karina helped her climb into the blue jumpsuit, with the Blue Horizons emblem stitched onto the right shoulder and an American flag displayed on the left. She could hardly hold the child still long enough to help her button the suit and adjust her helmet. By the time she finished explaining how the intercom worked, it was time for takeoff.

"Place your feet on the pedals, but don't push. Just follow along with me," Karina said, remembering Martin's instructions on that ill-fated day when she first took off in *Jet Stream*. They were lined up for takeoff. "The throttle is on your left. It's the little knob. Place your hand on it as we go. The throttle gives us our power."

"I know all that," Penny said. "I have a video on how to fly this airplane. Martin gave it to me for my birthday last year."

Takeoff went smoothly. The plane lifted effortlessly from the water and sailed into the sky at nearly a thousand feet a minute. Trees quickly became small specks.

Normally, they would have leveled out at about 1500-feet, but Martin and Karina planned on giving Penny the full treatment. High flight came first; then came a low slow flight to St. Louis. The highlight came about halfway, when Martin led them up to 3000-feet for Karina to give Penny a chance at controlling the airplane.

"Oh, this is really cool!" Penny said, after Karina talked her through a 360-degree turn. "I wish we could stay here forever. I feel so free, like I rule the world."

"Sorry, but Martin just radioed for me to take over. We have a schedule to keep and a limited amount of fuel. You don't want to walk, do you?"

Penny sighed deeply. "I guess you're right, but I just hate the thought of returning to earth. Still, I'm getting a little tired. I don't know why. I slept so hard last night, and it's not even ten o'clock in the morning yet."

"You got up awfully early," Karina said quickly. She didn't want Penny to figure out what might be causing her recent bout of fatigue. Penny was too smart not to come up with the answer if allowed to dwell on the problem.

"Karina, I think it might be more than that." Penny spoke tentatively, as if she were feeling Karina out.

"What makes you say that?"

"Well, I heard Daddy and Mommy whispering behind my back the last couple of nights. Whenever they do that, I end up in the hospital again."

Penny's voice was small, controlled. Karina didn't know what to say. Her own voice might give something away, and she didn't want to ruin the rest of Penny's dream flight.

Finally, Karina said, "Oh, I don't know, honey. Let's not think about it right now. Look below, on your right. Got any idea what that might be?"

Penny pressed her nose to the windshield and gazed below. "The Missouri River?"

"You got it. Another fifteen minutes and we'll be landing." Karina relaxed; the distraction had worked.

For a few minutes, they flew in silence, Penny with her nose glued to the window, and Karina maneuvering the plane to give her the best possible view.

"Thanks, Karina, for everything. I would never have had this chance if you hadn't come to us." Then, Penny dropped a bombshell. "What do you think heaven is like?"

Penny spoke without ever taking her eyes from the window. Her voice remained steady but subdued, surrendering. However, it all but knocked the wind out of Karina.

"Oh, I don't know, beautiful and quiet," Karina said. "Why do you ask?"

"I think I'm going there soon. My real parents are there, just like yours. I've been dreaming about them a lot lately. Do you think dreams mean anything?"

"Maybe," Karina said slowly, matching Penny's quiet manner. "But you have a long life ahead of you, kid. I've always wanted a little sister, and now that I've got one, I'm not letting you get away."

"You think of me as a sister?" Excitement filled Penny's voice.

"I sure do."

The revelation surprised Karina. She found it was true. She thought of the little muffin sitting in front of her as a sister.

"That's great." Penny turned and looked over the seat at Karina. "I think of you as a sister, too."

Karina switched her radio to intercom only. She didn't want Martin overhearing her next words. He might not approve.

"We're about ten minutes out now. Take the controls. The plane is yours for the next seven minutes."

Penny grabbed the controls, and Karina helped her fly the plane toward its final destination, Spirit of St. Louis Airport. No further words were spoken about heaven or lost parents.

Karina flew a flawless route into the airport. Cars and houses held dollhouse proportions, growing larger as the tiny plane descended. They had little wind and smooth sailing all the way. Penny delighted in every aspect of the landing and listened intently to each word Karina spoke. All too soon they landed, and Dr. and Mrs. Winfield told Penny the flight's true purpose.

Karina's heart broke. The little girl's expression never changed a bit. She simply turned from her parents afterwards and went to Karina. She put her small arms around Karina's waist, hugged her tightly, and thanked her for fulfilling her greatest dream.

Her parents, Martin, and Karina should have been consoling Penny, but quite the opposite happened. Penny consoled them. She reminded them that this operation was her chance for a full, normal life. If things went wrong, she wanted them to know how happy she was at this moment, and that if she had a choice, she would choose the operation. With her dream fulfilled, she was ready for anything. Holding hands, Penny led her mother and Karina to the car for the remaining drive to the hospital.

* * *

Karina paced relentlessly during the operation. She had spent a horrible night, tossing and turning. She hadn't eaten and hardly spoke to anyone, even Dr. and Mrs. Winfield. Everyone seemed to respect her silence, for no one interrupted.

After what seemed an eternity and two lifetimes, a doctor dressed in blue surgical scrubs came out to inform them that Penny was doing well at the moment, but it would be a couple of days before they knew if the operation was successful or not.

Martin said they had to be going. They were already late, and a bad weather pattern was heading into the Midwest. After a lengthy discussion, Karina was allowed to stay until the results were known. Martin, Sally, and the rest of the Blue Horizons team would head toward Oklahoma and into the Texas panhandle. Dr. Winfield would drive Karina to meet them as soon as they knew anything definite.

So, the long waiting game began. Penny stayed in the hospital until the results were determined. Karina never left her side. Dr. Winfield arranged for a semi-private room so Penny and Karina could be together. Mrs. Winfield spent all day with them, but left Penny in Karina's care at night.

Penny was very weak at first, but by the end of the third day, she was back to being her old self, anxious to leave the hospital. At last came the long-awaited results. Promising, the doctors said; maybe a complete success.

During Penny's convalescence, Karina and the Winfields kept close track of Blue Horizons. Television coverage became a nightly event now that they were rapidly crossing the United States. But also reported each night was news about serious weather cyclones building in the Atlantic Ocean and the Gulf of Mexico. All along the coast, people were heading inland.

The evening after the doctor's qualified report of success, Martin called and reported that Megan was ill with a severe ear infection. She couldn't fly, and they needed Karina back at once. If they were to get away from the Gulf Coast, she would have to reach them quickly. So after tearful good byes, Dr. Winfield packed her into the station wagon for a hasty dash southward. Driving through the night, they caught up with the Blue Horizons team outside of Amarillo—just in time, because the sky was already beginning to darken at eleven o'clock in the morning.

Less than an hour later, with the southern sky becoming night in the middle of the day, they took off against the eerie dark background, heading west toward New Mexico. The wind was strangely still, biding its time. They had to leave at once or sit it out for days, maybe weeks. Such a delay might end the journey, but as she guided her ultralight skyward, Karina wondered if it was possible to outrun such a weather system.

Chapter 10

Pressed into Service

Rain pounded on her canopy. Karina squinted through the blur at Devon, who was directing her towards the dock that was to be her tie-down point. They had landed on the Elephant Butte Reservoir, a little north of Truth or Consequences, New Mexico. This was how they had been traveling for the last eight days, ever since two major storm systems had swept across the Gulf Coast and slammed into Texas and Mexico. Identifying dozens of emergency landing sites, often in miserably wet conditions, the ground crew leap-frogged ahead each morning, long before daylight. The flight team took to the air between heavy squalls when the wind died down enough for safe flight.

The usually dry Southwest was deluged with water. Large portions of Texas were flooded from rivers swollen by more than thirty inches of rain. Two large hurricanes had swept into the Gulf of Mexico, hitting only days apart. Every newspaper reported this as a history-making weather system. Rampaging waters from streams that once only trickled had swamped whole towns.

In New Mexico, Karina flew over endless miles of flooded desert. The Rio Grande and Pecos Rivers, usually calm little rivers in which tourists could find comfort from relentless desert sunshine, had flooded thousands of desert acres and hundreds of homes. Rising water had also covered many roads, leaving whole communities isolated from basic services. Rumor had it that the National Guard and Civil Air Patrol were being called into service to help reach isolated areas.

"Come on. We've got hot cocoa waiting," Devon yelled. He had finished tying up *Meadow Lark* and offered Karina a hand. Rain whipped around them, and a wind gust practically lifted Karina off the ground. "Martin says we're probably going to be here a few days."

"What's the up-to-date weather forecast?" Karina asked. She knew there was a chance that yet another major storm was heading into the Gulf. She certainly hoped it would die out first. This fly and wait, and wait, and wait, was wearing thin on her nerves. More often than not, it was get ready and forget it, rather than preflight and fly. She was even current with all of her schoolwork, including algebra.

"Not good," Devon yelled. They ran to the command tent. "Things look bad, another full-fledged hurricane. That makes three."

All motels and other solid structures were already crowded with refugees from the storms, so the Blue Horizons team slept, worked and ate under wall tents. It was a real drag. Everything was covered with mud, making daily laundry essential. Cooking and eating became drudgeries best forgotten, and sightseeing was impossible.

The kids froze when rain fell and the wind blew, but as soon as the rain stopped and sun appeared, the temperature became uncomfortably hot, and muggy.

"Hurricane Carlos hit about an hour ago." Devon lifted the tent flap for Karina. "We could be here a few days. I think Martin's worried."

"I hope he doesn't cancel the trip," she said, ducking under the flap into the relative dryness inside.

"Here, Rini." Joe handed her a cup of cocoa. He had been first in formation, so he had landed a full ten minutes ahead of her. "Martin wants to talk with us in a little while. He said to stay under shelter. We're being driven into Truth or Consequences for the night. We'll be camping out in a Lutheran church."

Karina gratefully accepted the hot cocoa. "Where's Martin now? I want to find a phone. I haven't heard from Penny in over a week. He promised I could call today."

They sat at a card table where Sam and Katie played a game of chess, the favored pastime. Jessica and Paul sat on a bench listening to the weather radio, and all of the other students occupied themselves as best they could. The smell of mildew from days of dampness tainted the air inside the tent.

"He and some military fellow left a few minutes ago." Joe sipped steaming cocoa from his cup. "Said he'd be back in an hour or so, and we are to relax until he returns. There's no phone near here, and the cell phones aren't working very well. You'll probably have to wait until this evening."

Karina nodded, looking at her watch. It was only three-eighteen in the afternoon. She had time. Besides, she wasn't overly concerned. The last she'd heard, Penny was doing well, and everyone expected a full recovery. Martin promised her a week's vacation with the Winfields when they finished the flight to California, but with their current progress, it would take at least another month, maybe late August, before their cross-country odyssey concluded.

Joe brought a chessboard, and they spent the next few hours in friendly competition. Karina was new to chess, so Joe always won. But he also taught her much about the game and never gloated about winning.

Martin arrived a little before six o'clock with Mr. Smithson and a tall, slender man wearing a military uniform. An officer, Karina guessed. He seemed young, maybe in his late twenties, and towered over Martin.

"Everybody, this is Major Renford of the New Mexico National Guard. He's got a proposition for us. I'd like you to gather round and hear him out," Martin said.

He didn't have to ask twice. Less than a minute later, every member, students and staff, sat in a semicircle around Major Renford. Whatever this man had to say was certain to affect them, one way or another.

"Pleased to meet you," the Major said. "I've been following your progress ever since you left New York. In fact, it was the televised coverage of the Civil Air Patrol exercise in which you participated that brings me here."

The Major paused, looked at Martin, and then said, "I've been asked, as the military authority in this area, to evacuate stranded flood victims to safety. With the new storm dumping inches of rain on already saturated soil, we're going to have even greater flooding in this area, and that is the reason I'm here now. I've received permission from my superiors to impress any and all civilian help possible, which brings me to you."

Nervous, excited conversation broke out among the group, stalling Major Renford's next words. He waited patiently, as though he were used to working with teens. Even Martin waited for them to settle down, which took several long minutes.

The Major said, "I've talked with Captain Elliot from the Civil Air Patrol, and he has volunteered his entire wing into our service, but we don't have enough spotters. We need qualified persons to ride with the C.A.P. pilots and search for anyone on the ground who might need help. It seems to me that a group with your qualifications is the perfect choice. What do you say?"

A hush came over the group, but it was short-lived. Everyone volunteered. Certainly, they would help. But they also had questions for the Major and Martin.

Joe spoke first. "Would we fly as well? We're pretty good pilots."

Katie asked, "What about our flight to California. Is it over?" This was directed at Martin.

Jenny wanted to know, "Will we continue as ground crew, or will we have a chance to be in the air?"

It was Mr. Smithson who began the answers. "Some of you may have a chance to fly our planes when the weather breaks, but most of the time you'll be spotting in a Civil Air Patrol plane. Their planes can fly in rougher weather than our ultralights, and their pilots are all instrument qualified. Something with which you have no experience."

"Also, the C.A.P. pilots have experience with flying at night," Martin said. "That allows for longer search patterns. Our most experienced pilots, those who have flown our planes out here, may help search in the ultralights if we have stable, clearing weather. We don't want you flying across broken skies in this changeable weather. Your safety is still our prime concern. Besides, it helps no one if we have to stop rescue efforts to search for you because you've been forced down by sudden adverse weather conditions."

Martin also answered Jenny's question. "Mr. Smithson and the Blue Horizons staff, myself included, have decided to finish our cross-country flight even if it takes until the end of September. You've worked too long and hard not to finish. In my opinion, the practical knowledge of the next few days will be far more valuable than a few more classroom days at Mitchum Field."

Everyone nodded agreement on that comment, and questions continued for the next half hour before everyone was satisfied. Martin, to everyone's surprise, held the rank of Colonel in the United States Air Force Reserve. He would fly a National Guard helicopter. Sally and a C.A.P. pilot would take turns flying a Cessna 182, a four-seat airplane. The rest of the group would be split up among the C.A.P. as spotters, at least until the weather stabilized.

By the time the meeting concluded and the Blue Horizons kids were headed into Truth or Consequences for food, showers and a good night's rest, all students had been assigned a flight schedule.

Everyone, except Karina and Jessica, was assigned duty with a C.A.P. pilot. Karina and Jessica would fly with Martin in a National Guard helicopter. The other kids envied them, but none complained. The job they were called on to fulfill was far too important for petty rivalries.

It was hard getting to sleep, even though everyone obeyed Martin's no-talking rule. They camped out together in a Lutheran church. The National Guard provided cots for their comfort, but everyone was restless, tossing and turning.

Karina called the Winfields and learned that Penny was doing well. The girl talked Karina's ear off when she heard Karina was going to take part in a real rescue effort. Only Martin's negotiated settlement, and insistence that Karina really needed to get some rest, pried Penny from the phone.

The next two days brought about flight after flight. Most of the time, the kids spotted people and notified proper authorities who responded with boat rescues. They flew from sunrise to sundown, stopping only for rainsqualls that grounded them several times a day. The days were long, in the air by six o'clock every morning and down just before sunset on days when the sun was out. Then it was dinner, briefing for the next day's search pattern and bed.

Karina and Jessica had it a little better with Martin in the helicopter, or "chopper" as Martin called it. At some places, they were able to land and pick up stranded victims. Other times, they hauled food, water, blankets and medicine to people cut off from supplies, but not in immediate danger from rising water.

"Snap it up," Martin said. "A news helicopter crew has spotted a small church with a dozen or more people stranded on the roof." He moved to the counter and grabbed a sandwich and Styrofoam cup filled with hot coffee. "We're the only ones available who can get to them before dark," he said between mouthfuls.

Karina shoved the last of a tuna salad sandwich into her mouth and gulped her soda. "Should we stow aboard extra blankets in case we can't get them all out before dark?" She grabbed her own jacket and tossed Jessica her poncho.

"Good idea, but don't take long. It's more important to get there." Martin was already leaving. "We've got food and water on board. We don't want much more. It'll cut down on how many people we can rescue at a time."

They hurried to the helicopter, loaded half a dozen blankets, and strapped themselves into flight seats. Martin and Jessica sat up front in the pilot and copilot seats. Karina rode shotgun in back. Actually, she liked it better back there. The doors had been removed from this helicopter, and the wind blew wildly through her hair sneaking out beneath her flight helmet. The noise was so loud, they had to yell to one another to be heard, so they wore helmets with intercom radios attached.

Karina found riding in front boring when she couldn't take the controls. Martin had laughed at her when she confided that revelation to him the previous night, and he told her she was now a real pilot. She took his remark as a compliment.

"Karina, put on the safety line and look below." Martin's metallic voice echoed through her headset. He began circling a small cluster of trees, their tops only a few feet above the murky, swirling flood waters. "I thought I saw something red in the treetops."

Martin circled the area slowly while Karina fastened herself into the safety harness. She took her time and double-checked each buckle. The harness, attached to a thin, shiny steel rescue cable, was all that separated her from the devastation below. Without it, one slip might be fatal. Even her full life jacket might not be enough to keep her safe in the water. Undercurrents, fence posts, and other submerged objects could force her under water. The thought made her queasy, so she returned to the task at hand and fastened the cable snugly into a metal rung bolted to the helicopter's floorboard. This setup allowed her to step onto the runner and look directly below.

"I don't see anything," she said into her microphone. Unlike her intercom in *Jet Stream*, this one was voice activated. She didn't need to press the button to speak. Suddenly, a speck of red blinked at her from between dense green tree branches. "Wait a minute. Swing left and come around. There's something in the top of one of the trees."

Martin did as she directed, and the helicopter hovered over what looked like a red-and-white tablecloth. Karina pulled her goggles down to keep the wind out and focus better.

"Hey, Martin!" she said, hardly believing what she saw. "There're three people down there. Looks like one woman and a couple of kids. Can't tell how old. What do we do? They don't look too secure."

"Can you get a line down to them from the hoist? I'll send Jessica to help if it's possible. I've already radioed in a report, but there aren't any boats in this vicinity."

Karina wasn't sure. The hoist system consisted of a small electric winch motor bolted to the floor with a line running through a pulley fastened to the upper hatchway. She certainly didn't want to get the hoist's cable caught in one of the trees. Martin had warned that snagging a tree was the fastest way to bring them down. When helicopters lost control, they frequently lost lift and fell quickly. She tightened the three heavy-duty web straps that secured her life jacket and the metal fastener that locked her safety harness in place.

"I don't know," she said. "We can try, but it's going to be tricky. The trees are really dense, and the limbs don't look too sturdy." Karina's heart pumped vigorously and her hands were sweaty, but she dutifully fastened on a rescue harness and swung the hook out and away from the side, just above the frantically waving victims beneath her.

By the time the hoist line began its descent, Jessica had fastened herself in behind Karina. Together, they watched the lady desperately pushing the two children up among the limber treetop branches.

The water was higher than Karina had first thought. The lady must have been partly submerged, allowing the two children a higher perch.

Jessica patted the top of Karina's helmet, the agreed signal that she was supporting Karina. From her secured position, Jessica's job was to pull the rescued person into the helicopter because Karina was actually standing outside on the helicopter's landing runners so she could better judge where the line was and help direct it toward the struggling figures below.

"Line's headed down," she said to Martin. The thump, thump, thump of the helicopter's rotors blew down around her, sending waves of water rippling in all directions. A seat harness was attached to the end of the line. It fastened around a person's waist and legs and guarded against falling while being hauled up.

Though Karina's vision was limited, she thought the woman was having a rough time trying to get the first child into the harness. The struggling child might never have been secured, if the second child hadn't joined in to help. Karina saw the second child, who was somewhat bigger than the child being forced into the harness, grab hold of the smaller figure, giving the woman just enough time to fasten the necessary straps and swing the child away from her, away from any danger of being snagged by a tree branch.

Immediately, Karina began reeling up the line. First to arrive from the treetops, was a little five- or six-year-old boy. He cried and kicked so hard that it took Jessica several minutes to haul him in.

"Swing him this way," Jessica said to Karina, who was in a position behind the hysterical boy. "Push hard and I can pin him to the floor."

Karina followed her friend's directions to the letter, giving the child a mighty shove. He swung into Jessica's arms, and she wrestled him to the floor and slipped him from the harness.

"Hang on. I'll give you a hand." Karina climbed into the helicopter. "Hold his arms and I'll get his legs."

Together, Karina and Jessica overpowered the boy and slid him to a metal bench that served as a seat on the military-style helicopter. After another short struggle, they finally strapped him into one of the two bench seats that held three people each. Jessica wrapped a blanket around the soggy child, sat beside him on the bench, and hugged him tightly while Karina returned to her rescue position.

Next came a sturdy nine- or ten-year-old girl who only had to be coaxed inside. Afraid to look down, the child wouldn't move until Karina shoved the cable in close enough for the girl's feet to reach the helicopter floor.

"We've got the two kids, and the line's going down for their mom," Karina said to her instructor. "Better let them know the boat won't be necessary."

"Roger," Martin said. "What shape are our passengers in?"

Karina quickly surveyed Jessica's efforts with the children and glanced down at the lady struggling to strap on the harness Karina had lowered. "They're cold and tired, but I don't think they need any medical attention. Jessica has the two kids fastened into one of the bench seats with a blanket wrapped around each child. I'm working on their mom now."

A few minutes later, Karina and a very grateful mother rolled onto the floor of the helicopter. The lady was soaking wet, her teeth chattering. She tried to thank her rescuers but only chattering teeth could be heard. Karina and Jessica helped her into a seat and provided her with a wool army blanket.

"Thank you, so much. We've been clinging to those trees since early this morning," the mother said, then noticed the age of her rescuers. "Why, you're just children."

Jessica offered hot cocoa from a thermos. "Yes, ma'am. We're students from Blue Horizons, an alternative school that teaches flying. The pilot is one of our instructors." She answered the woman's next question before it could be asked. "My name's Jessica, and this is Karina."

Karina finished battening down the hoist and sat on the bench across from the woman and her children.

"Everyone's on board," Karina said to Martin. "Better head for the church. We can still handle three or four more, if Jessica and I sit on the floor." She turned toward the woman. "Ma'am, you don't mind if we pick up a few more people, do you? I know you must really want to get back."

The lady smiled and shook her head. "Name's Maggie. This is Karen and Bobby." She pointed to her children as she spoke their names. "Rescue as many as you can. We certainly know what it means to see help on the way. We were so afraid you wouldn't see us. Two other planes and another helicopter flew by, but they didn't see us waving."

On route to the church, the children calmed down, but none could get over the fact their rescuers were children. By the time the church was in sight, Karina and Jessica had explained Blue Horizons and how they happened to be on board a National Guard helicopter.

"I've got the church in sight, better get strapped in again, Karina," Martin said a few minutes later. "I make out fourteen. That means two more trips. We'd better hurry if we're going to make it before dark."

Karina strapped herself in and began hauling up victims as soon as Martin was over the church. Without any trees to snag, this rescue went faster. As Maggie had done, the group clustered on the church roof sent children up first.

After Karina and Jessica hauled the fourth child on board, Martin made a quick run back. Maggie made the girls promise to look her up at the end of the day. She wanted to thank them again and hear more about their cross-country flight.

Back at the landing site, Karina and Jessica hurriedly helped the children into the waiting arms of Red Cross workers. Maggie waved a final good bye, and once again the helicopter streaked above the flooded desert countryside.

The second trip to the church was uneventful. Up came four women and two men without incident. Only the routine explanation about how children came to be their rescuers provided any challenge, which was good, for both Karina and Jessica were fatigued from the long, emotionally draining day.

"Looks like someone's beat us," Martin said on their third arrival at the church. They hoped to collect the last four flood victims before dark. However, as they closed in, a blue-and-white helicopter with CNC News painted on its side was already lowering a rope to the remaining victims.

"They better watch out," Karina said. The two men in the news helicopter were using rope instead of cable, and the flexible rope whipped around considerably more than cable did.

"National Guard helicopter to CNC News team." Martin tried to relay Karina's warning. "You're in danger of snagging the steeple. Move away. We'll take over. Do you copy? Over."

Karina couldn't tell if they heard or not. Immediately after Martin's call, the rope wrapped around the steeple and jerked the helicopter sideways. The pilot lost control and the helicopter spiraled into the rushing floodwater. Everything happened so fast; Karina didn't even have time to yell. She was stunned.

Jessica found words first. "Martin, they're down. Two in the water. I don't see anyone else. What should we do?"

"Hang on," Martin yelled. "We're going down close. Get Karina strapped in. We'll follow them downstream if we can. Go after the one without a life jacket first."

Martin swung the helicopter closer to the water, so that Karina wouldn't have far to lower the cable. They were flying only a few feet above the churning water. Three times, Karina tried to get a line to the man, but he was so tired from struggling against the undertow that he didn't have the strength to climb into the harness. He clung on for a while, but always slipped away.

Without thinking about the ramifications, Karina released herself from the safety of her own secured harness and fastened herself into the one attached to the rescue cable, hit the emergency release, and stepped away from the runner. Instantly, she dropped into the cold murky water below, about four feet away from the exhausted pilot.

The drop plunged Karina several feet under the water. Kicking hard and pulling with her arms, and aided by the buoyancy of her life jacket, her head emerged from the muddy water at the same time her breath gave out. Gasping for air, she swam toward her objective. Karina knew he was using the last of his energy just to remain above the water's surface.

Wearing both harness and life jacket, Karina had trouble swimming. Her initial entry and swim to the surface drained vital energy. Her flight suit filled with water, and the helmet weighed her head down, but through sheer willpower she reached the pilot and wrapped her arms and legs tightly around him. She worried that he'd panic and take them both under, but he was too fatigued to even hold on. He would have been gone if she'd reached him a few seconds later.

At the same moment that Karina caught hold of the man, Jessica started the winch. Karina's arms and legs closed around the pilot's limp body. Slowly and steadily, Karina felt the hoist lift them from the water. Karina looked up and saw Jessica standing on the runner. She knew Jessica hated standing outside the bouncing helicopter, the wind beating on her from the ever-thumping rotors. She saw Jessica's legs shaking from fear and the strain of balancing on the bouncing runner. She could almost feel how desperately Jessica wanted to climb inside the helicopter to safety. Karina also knew that Jessica wouldn't desert her, knew that Jessica wouldn't let her best friend down.

It took every ounce of Karina's strength to maintain her grip on her lifeless victim. Fortunately, he was a small man, not much taller than she was. Nevertheless, he was about 60-pounds heavier. She didn't have a very good grip with her arms, but her quavering legs were locked tightly around his waist.

Rising above the water made matters worse. Karina now carried a dead weight. She didn't even know whether he was still breathing.

"Please, God, let him be alive," she prayed softly while the hoist inched closer to the helicopter's runner. Squeezing her legs as hard as possible, her muscles screaming in torment and her ankles locked together, Karina felt the man starting to slip from her.

"Help, I'm losing him." Karina's voice held a note of panic. She tightened her arms and closed her eyes, unaware that Jessica was only an arm's length away.

Jessica grabbed the line and pulled with all her weight and strength, like a marlin fisherman pulling in a trophy-sized catch. The man stirred and tried to help, but his arms seemed useless, moving in slow uncoordinated arcs. At least he was still alive, still breathing.

Karina found her feet on the helicopter's runners. The man was between her and the door. She gave a final shove and he landed on top of Jessica before rolling over and slamming into the seat.

Shaking from exertion, ushering up more determination than Karina thought possible, she left him to Jessica. She had another man still in the water. At least this one wore a life jacket. She climbed into her secured safety harness and sent the line down while Jessica worked behind her.

"We've got one," she said to Martin in a weak voice. She knew he'd be furious with her later for such a foolish stunt, but figured she'd cross that bridge when she came to it. "The other's below us, about fifty yards ahead."

Martin moved in for the second man, while Jessica dealt with the pilot. Not only was he cold and wet, but he also had a nasty gash above his left eyebrow. Blood flowed in a slow steady stream from the injury. Karina watched from the corner of her eye as Jessica applied a pressure bandage. Karina was grateful for the emergency first aid training that was part of Blue Horizon's curriculum.

Once again, Karina checked to make sure she was securely attached to the helicopter. She had no desire to go back into the water. Her legs shaking from their previous exertion, she wasn't sure she had enough strength to pull in another victim.

"He's right below us," she said to Martin. "The line is going down now."

This time the rescue went according to procedure. In little more than two minutes, the second man, the reporter, was safely deposited onto the helicopter's floor space between the two seats.

"We've got two," Karina said to Martin. "You can head back now."

Twenty minutes, and four additional rescue pickups later, Karina worked her way forward to sit by Martin. She slid into the copilot's seat with a resigned sigh. Whatever Martin had to say, she would have to take it. She was too tired to put up a struggle.

"Everyone okay back there?" asked Martin. He waited for her to reply before saying more. They were heading to the landing pad and had about fifteen minutes to sort things out.

"The pilot's going to need a doctor. He's got a bad laceration above his left eye and maybe a concussion," she said. "Jessica's working on him, and the reporter guy's helping. They were lucky to get out of their helicopter before it went under. I've never seen anything drop so fast."

"There are two things helicopters don't do well," said Martin. "Glide and float. You know, that was a pretty brave stunt you pulled back there."

"I thought you'd say it was dumb," Karina said, surveying a large bruise forming on her forearm where she'd banged it against the side of the helicopter while trying to get the pilot on board. "Are you angry with me?"

"Certainly." Martin lined up for the final approach to the landing pad. "But I'm awfully proud, also. You took ten years off my life when you went into the water. But I've been in the business of commanding people in tough situations before. I try to set aside what the consequences could have been. There's too much emotion involved. We'll discuss that part later."

Martin made a nifty little maneuver and settled the helicopter onto the makeshift landing pad. "I've also been around long enough to know real heroism when I see it. What you did was very brave and selfless. That pilot owes you his life."

Karina hadn't thought about her actions, either before or afterwards, in the kind of depth Martin was laying out. She didn't feel like a hero. Tears began running from her eyes, brought about from pent up emotion and Martin's unexpected kindness. She'd done what had to be done. How could she live with herself if she'd stood by and watched someone drown without even attempting to help? She said so to Martin while he killed the engine. She also told him how frightened she was when she hit the water, and again on the runner, pulling in the reporter.

The victims quickly disembarked and Jessica popped up front to check on Karina. Martin politely asked her to leave, saying he and Karina were discussing some things. Jessica didn't have to be told twice. She told Karina she was going to get cleaned up and would wait for her so they could have dinner together. They had promised to have dinner with Maggie and her children.

After Jessica's departure, Martin said. "Karina, heroes are people who are forced to act because of a situation thrust upon them. They do so selflessly and sometimes at great personal risk. Your action was impulsive, and could have had dire results, but your desire to help a human being in desperate need is highly commendable."

Karina listened carefully. She wasn't exactly sure how she felt. It had been a very demanding day, and another one might be only hours away. Wiping the last trace of tears from her eyes, she wanted to forget about being in the water. All she wanted was a long hot bath, something to eat and sleep.

Martin hesitated, then said. "I can see how tired you are, and you need to get out of those wet clothes, so we'll finish this talk another time." He reached out and gently turned her head so she looked him straight in the eyes. "If you do anything else like that without first consulting with me, this trip will be over for you. Not just the rescue work. The whole trip. Understand?"

"Yes, sir." Karina stared into firm, but kind eyes. "I understand. Believe me. I have no intention of ever going into floodwater again."

"That's not exactly what I mean," said Martin. "Get out of here, now!"

Karina didn't wait for another word. She was in Truth or Consequences a short time later. After a long relaxing shower—there wasn't a bathtub available—she joined Jessica for dinner.

Maggie, who turned out to be one of the largest ranch owners in the county, had reservations at a local restaurant. She treated them to dinner and talked about Karina's rescue for over an hour. Jessica swore to Karina that she hadn't informed Maggie about Karina's wild leap into floodwater. Maggie pointed out that it's pretty difficult to save a television reporter without the whole world knowing about it.

After Maggie and the kids thanked Jessica and Karina again, the girls headed for bed, only to find news reporters waiting for them. It took almost another hour before they finally reached the bed's quiet sanctuary.

Martin stopped by and told both girls that they were to report to him first thing in the morning. He said things were getting worse down in Texas and southeastern New Mexico, down on the Pecos River. He was going to allow them to take to the air and help National Guard ground and boat teams. Water was still rising and another weather system was building in the Gulf. They had to get everyone out before it built into another hurricane.

Karina and Jessica felt honored. It would be just the two of them and Joe. Megan and Paul would work with Martin. Sally was in charge. Working a hundred miles away from Martin would seem strange. They would be more on their own than ever before.

That night, Karina had another nightmare. However, this time it wasn't her father's plane crash. She dreamed of being trapped in her ultralight in the dark, bouncing up and down with a storm crashing all around. Only, she wasn't flying. This time, the plane was sitting on the water. As the storm grew in intensity, Karina woke up. She felt ill and staggered to the bathroom.

After losing most of her fabulous meal, Karina climbed into bed, shaking uncontrollably. She didn't have a fever, and she didn't think she was afraid of flying. She wasn't exactly sure what she felt, but inside, she knew something was wrong. It was an uneasy sleep that won her over, twisting and turning, as the plane bounced up and down on turbulent waters.

Chapter 11

▼

Broken Skies

"Karina, you and Joe swing northwest over this area here," Sally said in a final briefing. They used a corner of the local sheriff's station as their briefing room to organize their search pattern. "Jessica and I will swing over the sector southwest of your position, and we'll meet here for the flight back."

Two days had passed since Karina's nightmare, and nothing dramatic had happened. The trip from Truth or Consequences had proved uneventful. The only major complication was 20-hours of continuous rain after they arrived. The heavy rainfall dumped another 22-inches of water onto the flooded desert plain. Now, clouds were beginning to break up, and the searchers were going to chance a broad two-sector sweep.

"Remember to follow your Ground Positioning System—GPS—all the way," Sally said. "We don't want to be searching for you, so let's not become part of the problem, all right?"

They all agreed and gathered their flight gear. The C.A.P. was overloaded with rescue work, and this area had, for the most part, not been searched because just southeast of them, across the border into Texas, conditions were immeasurably worse.

Karina quickly preflighted *Jet Stream*. She was flying the two-seat ultralight today. Its greater range and power made it more effective, but her instructions were to stay with Joe. They would work as a team.

Minutes before noon, all four planes took off and joined in formation over endless miles of flooded desert. They flew west together for the first twenty minutes. Then, Sally and Jessica started their circle southward, while Karina and Joe turned north.

"See anything?" Joe asked over the radio. "I haven't spotted anything, but some bloated cattle snagged in that bunch of treetops we passed 30-miles back. Over."

"No, nothing, but muddy water and a few dead animals," Karina said. "Can you believe this scene? If I didn't know we were flying above what was normally desert, I wouldn't believe it. Except for some small hilltop islands, there's no dry land for miles. Let's swing left, over toward those mountains. There ought to be pockets of dry land there. Over."

Karina called Joe an hour later. He was flying her favorite plane. "*Jet Stream* to *Meadow Lark*. Better begin your turn eastward and watch your fuel. I'm going to follow that ridgeline a little farther west. Looks like submerged houses on the horizon. Over." She banked westward.

"I'll go with you," Joe said, duplicating Karina's move. "Sally won't like you being that far out alone. Over."

Joe was right. Sally wouldn't like her going alone, but her ten-gallon gas tank gave her twice the fuel that the single-seat ultralights held. Her extra fuel capacity made the longer search safe for her, but Joe would be flying on fumes, pushing his safety margin to the limit. Sally would like that less, and Joe knew it. He was just trying to be protective again. Every since Karina had told him about her nightmare, he had hovered around her like a mother hen.

"Thanks, Joe," she said over the radio. "But you don't have enough fuel to stay with me. I'll be fine. I'm just going to take a quick look. I'll catch up before you reach Sally and Jessica. Over."

Joe mumbled that he still didn't like it but swung eastward, parting with a warning to be careful. With both planes flying in opposite directions, they lost sight of each other in no time.

Karina turned her attention ahead, to what appeared to be water-covered farm or ranch houses about 30-miles, farther west. She saw plenty of water below her where swollen streams encircled higher land outcrops, creating a desolate scene of islands and muddy channels of swift-moving water. She flew west along the dingy grayish-green ridgeline, scanning for life, but found none. She flew above bloated cows floating in stagnant backwater where the swirling current had deposited them. Karina hated the thought of those poor animals, frightened, with nowhere to turn, swimming frantically, only to sink exhausted beneath the cold, murky water. Even more, she dreaded the possibility of encountering human victims of the merciless killer raging below. Minute, after long minute, she circled the area.

With her fuel gauge reading less than half, and time running out, Karina began a 180-degree turn. "Wait a minute," she said to herself. Something was moving, maybe waving. "What's that? I knew it. There is something out there."

She swung back again, heading toward a mostly submerged building with two small blobs on top. She had time for only one quick pass. A longer search might exceed her range and endanger a safe return. She'd already stayed longer than planned. Sally, Joe, and Jessica were probably flying eastward at this very moment.

Closer to the buildings, she saw the two figures on top were pretty small. Maybe they were children, but maybe not. They waved at her in long movements with blankets, first above their heads, and then down, all the way to the roof. She rocked her wings up and down, letting them know she'd seen them and help was on the way, but the small figures continued waving without any letup until they were out of her sight.

Karina checked her GPS and marked the location on her kneeboard. If boats were available, they might be able to reach the area before dark. The sky was darkening to the south again, and the ceiling was closing in above her. Soon, there would be more rain.

* * *

When Karina landed, Sally was waiting for her. "Get out of your flight suit and join me in the briefing room at once," Sally said loudly. Then, she abruptly turned and departed, not waiting for Karina to respond.

Karina could see Sally was really angry. With only a nod, she followed Sally's directions. Sally was always so quiet. Karina had never heard her raise her voice before.

"Flying alone is strictly forbidden. What possible reason justified breaking safety rules?" Sally asked, slamming her fist on the desk for emphasis when Karina entered the room. It was deserted except for Sally and herself. Obviously, everyone knew it was a good time to be somewhere else.

"I saw rooftops in the distance as Joe and I came to the end of our search pattern," Karina said. "I had a feeling people were there, and I had enough fuel. I wanted them to know they'd been spotted, and Joe didn't have enough fuel to stay with me. I located two people on a rooftop, probably children. I didn't see any adults. Here are the coordinates."

Sally took the coordinates and noted them on her board. When she spoke again, her voice was softer, less threatening. "Karina, this information is certainly useful, but I can't have you risking your safety. From now on, you'll fly with me. Joe will work with Jessica. Now, get out of here. Go get something to eat."

"What about the children?" Karina asked. "Will someone reach them before it gets dark?"

"I'll give your coordinates to the authorities, but the wind's picking up. A new storm front is headed our way. It might be late tomorrow before rescuers arrive in Delta Sector." Sally placed the note on the sheriff's desk. As chief of emergency operations for this quadrant, the sheriff dictated where and when rescue teams were deployed. "Get out. The kids will think I'm beating you or something."

Karina wanted to argue, but knew it was out of Sally's control. Well, she'd eat, and then see if the sheriff acted on her tip. Sally and Jessica had found a large group of people cut off in an area of rapidly rising water. They would have first priority.

"Hey, Amelia," Joe said. Every time she did something he considered dangerous, he jokingly compared her to Amelia Earhart, the famous aviator lost trying to fly across the Pacific Ocean. "You trying for a solo around the world, or what?"

"Not funny," she said. "I'm not trying for any records, and I didn't like the hero junk I had to put up with after that news helicopter fiasco." She joined Jessica and Joe at the small Pizza Hut table.

"What's up?" asked Jessica, handing a cold Pepsi to Karina. "Sally yell at you? She was furious when Joe showed up alone. She didn't ground you, did she?"

Karina shook her head. "No, but I'm her permanent partner. You and Joe are flying together. That's not what's bothering me. I spotted some people on a rooftop at the far western end of Delta Sector. I think they're kids, and Sally doubts anyone can get there before the storm hits. They were frantically waving, like more was wrong than just being stranded."

The lady at the counter brought their order, two large pepperoni pizzas smothered in onions.

"The weather report says the storm should hit sometime after sunset," said Joe, helping himself to a large slice. "Are you sure they're children?"

"Pretty sure," she said. Everyone munched pizza, talking with full mouths. They continued discussing the situation while they ate, until there wasn't a single slice of pizza remaining.

"Well, one thing is certain, we won't be doing anything about it." Joe slid pizza crust around his plate. They had eliminated every possible solution for mounting a rescue attempt.

Listening to the others, Karina became quiet as an idea formed. Would Joe and Jessica go along with it? Sally certainly wouldn't. Karina had seen only two people on that roof. They were not in immediate danger, but why would two children be alone? If they weren't children, they were certainly adults small enough to fit in the front seat of the two-seat ultralights.

She checked with the sheriff about the possibility of rescue that night. The sheriff informed her any rescue would have to wait for morning and safer weather. Frustrated, Karina brought the idea to Joe and Jessica. Her watch already read six-forty in the evening, and the sky was turning black south of them.

Both Joe and Jessica felt an evening rescue was too dangerous. They reasoned that if the children had been there this long, another night wouldn't put them in much greater jeopardy. Jessica felt Sally wouldn't go along with the idea.

Karina saw their logic. She excused herself, saying she had a headache and wanted to lie down for a while. She went to her bunk and tried to rest, but something about the strange way the children—she knew they were children—kept waving made her uncomfortable. She couldn't rest. A crazy idea kept running through her mind.

She looked at her watch. It now read a little past seven-thirty. If she left before eight, she could make it out and back before dark. If the storm held long enough, and if the two people were small enough to fit in one seat, she might make it. Too many ifs, but she had to try. She could bring at least one back.

Karina quickly slipped outside and fueled up *Jet Stream*. She thought about asking Joe or Jessica to fly *Blue Bird* along with her. That way, they'd surely be able to rescue both victims, but she didn't want to get her friends into trouble. She knew this would be her last flight for a long time, successful or not. But, it would be worth it if she could help those kids. Another night of misery, sitting out another storm, wondering if help was coming or not, might make the children desperate enough to try something crazy, like swimming to higher ground.

Something crazy, Karina thought as *Jet Stream* lifted off, swinging westward. What could be crazier than this? Sally was sure to have her head. Martin would probably ground her indefinitely, or worse. The storm was approaching as well as night. Was she just dumber than most, or was she really a troublemaker? Karina couldn't decide. She wanted to follow orders, and wanted to be praised, but somehow she always messed things up. That was her life all right, messed up. Yet, she had to make this rescue attempt, regardless of how others felt about her. She couldn't desert people in trouble, especially if those people turned out to be helpless children.

A strong wind gust bounced Karina about, reminding her to stop feeling sorry for herself and finish the task at hand. She had already burned her bridges, so to speak. What happened when she returned was going to happen, whether she rescued the kids or not, so she might as well finish what she started.

It was almost dark when Karina reached the children again. Strange, they were waving just as they had been before, only this time they waved in the opposite direction. It seemed as though they were concentrating on something else. She'd have to hurry. The rain-darkened sky meant daylight was in short supply.

Karina circled, checking for ripples on the stagnant water to help her identify wind direction. Then, she lined up and brought the ultralight down smoothly onto the water. She kept a sharp eye out. Debris lying just under the surface could lead to a catastrophe.

Nothing snagged her from underneath, and she guided her plane to the submerged house. She was correct. Two girls were on the flat corrugated metal rooftop. They had moved across to her side but were still swinging those blankets with all their might.

Karina gasped as she slid her plane up close to the roof. "Oh my Lord." She finally understood what the children were doing. The water around them teemed with snakes—rattlesnakes. The girls were trying to keep them from climbing onto the roof.

She raised her canopy window and locked it open. "Get ready to climb into the front seat. I'll swing alongside."

The girls obeyed immediately, and Karina swung the plane around so that the side touched the roof. Her wing allowed just enough clearance for the children to duck underneath. She killed her engine. The plane had plowed through the snakes, scattering them.

Better hurry, she thought. Karina unfastened her shoulder harness and seat belt. She stepped out to steady the plane, so the children could board.

The girls came running as soon as the plane stopped moving. They dashed underneath the wing, holding onto it to keep their balance. "Thank you. We knew you'd come," said the oldest child, tears streaming down her face. She appeared to be about ten or eleven. The other little girl couldn't have been older than seven or eight.

"Hurry, we don't have much time," Karina shouted. The plane's nose kept swinging away from the roof. She had to do something. There was a real danger of one of the kids falling into the water. Karina pulled hard on the wing with both hands, holding it steady. She kept a careful watch at her feet. Snakes slithered, hissing onto the roof, rattles buzzing a warning. "You'll both have to sit up front. Hurry!"

The oldest girl boosted the younger one over the side and into the front seat. Then, she jumped in herself, landing beside the smaller child. The unexpected jump shoved the plane's nose outward causing Karina to lose her balance. Her foot slipped. She took three quick steps backward to settle the plane. A red-hot needle sank into her upper right thigh as she hopped into the back seat.

"Ow!" she screamed. "Hurry! Get the door down and fasten it. Help me!" She glanced at the cause of her torment.

A large diamondback rattlesnake coiled next to the plane raised its rattle and vibrated it menacingly back and forth. Large, white, needle-sharp fangs struck against the cockpit door just as Karina and the oldest girl sealed it against the danger outside. A second earlier and the strike would have reached Karina's face. The plane drifted from the house, which already had a dozen or more snakes slithering across the roof.

Karina felt dizzy and nauseated. She leaned over and grabbed one of the many barf bags she always had handy. She opened it just in time. Her stomach heaved over and over uncontrollably. Fire inched up her right leg, which felt strangely tight in her flight suit.

"Hey, let's go. What's the matter?" The older girl turned around and looked at her from the front seat. "Did they get you?"

Karina opened her mouth to speak, but had to reach for the bag again as her only response. When she finished, she noticed she had also wet her pants. *Disgusting*, she thought. The pain in her leg increased and dark clouds of unconsciousness closed around her. Never before in Karina's memory had she felt such intense pain, even when her father's plane crashed.

"Lady, you've got to call for help!" Little hands reaching around the front seat draped a cold, wet cloth on Karina's forehead. "That's a bad bite. It must have been a big one. Lady?"

Karina forced her eyes to focus. She tried to shift her position. Pain immediately took control of her life and willed her immobile. Once again, the world started to dim, but this time, she fought back.

"Try not to move. I'm coming back." The older girl raised the canopy and climbed over the seat. There wasn't enough room with the canopy closed. Even with the canopy open, the girl could barely put her legs into the back cockpit area. She had to sit on the side of the ultralight, holding onto the canopy.

"No!" Karina protested. "The snakes might get in." Her mouth felt like dry cotton. Her words came out garbled.

The older girl reached down and slit Karina's pant leg open with a small pocketknife, exposing her right leg. It was already terribly swollen and bruised. A large puncture mark halfway down her thigh oozed blood. The little girl slipped off her T-shirt and wrapped it around Karina's leg above the bite. She tightened it some but not enough to cut off blood flow. The pain was unbearable.

"Please, don't," Karina said, panicking from fear and pain. "It hurts so bad. What about the snakes? Don't let them get in here with us."

"We've drifted from the house. That's where the snakes are," the girl said. "We've been beating them off the roof all day. I don't think we'd have been able to keep them off much longer. Our arms were wearing out, and we didn't have a flashlight."

Karina yelled as a muscle contraction in her thigh intensified the sharp burning pain. "Oh, it hurts!"

The girl used her knife to cut off Karina's right pant leg. "That should help a little, but we've got to get you help. Does your radio work, lady?"

"My name's Karina, not lady," she mumbled. The pain subsided a little, from unbearable to steady misery. "What's yours?"

"Tina, and my sister's name is Kelly," the child said. She took the cloth from Karina's forehead, dipped it into the water, and repositioned it above Karina's eyes. "What about the radio? Does it work?"

It was almost dark now, and rain was beginning to fall. Karina tried to use the radio, but received only static for her effort. She showed Tina how to use it, but the storm messed up their signal, providing nothing but static.

"Close the door," she said. "You're getting wet. You'll get sick."

Tina smiled at Karina. Having used her sister's shirt for the cloth on Karina's head and her own for the restricting band around her leg, both girls were bare to the waist, dressed only in denim shorts and sandals. However, the air temperature was still very warm, even against the cold rain.

"Okay, but we're fine. Just hungry and thirsty. We'll catch some rainwater to drink. Want some?"

The next hour seemed surreal to Karina. Tina and Kelly did their best to take care of her. They certainly weren't helpless children. The rain kept pouring and Karina felt worse. It was dark, and the plane bounced up and down on the water. Lightning lit up the sky every few seconds, and thunder made talking a chore.

Karina knew they had to wait out the night. She only hoped the storm would stop before morning. If not, it might be late afternoon, or even another day, before they were rescued. She'd really made a mess of things. She didn't think she could fly. But, if the rain stopped, at first light, she'd give it a try.

The bite was bad. She'd done a report on snakes for extra credit in biology. She knew that large western diamondback rattlesnakes were the second leading killer of snakebite victims in the United States—second only to the slightly larger eastern diamondbacks. Not too many people died each year, though, and she should have a chance if she got help soon enough.

However, the searing pain pulsating through her leg gave her no comfort. Her watch's illuminated dial told her the time was only nine-thirty, a little more than an hour since the bite. Her leg was swollen from knee to hip. She vomited every ten minutes or so, managing only "dry heaves" now. The one positive thing about the bite was that only a single fang had penetrated her leg. The other fang had struck her kneeboard.

Tina and Kelly devoured the large Hershey's chocolate bar Karina had brought with her. They gulped half of the two-liter water bottle contained in the plane's emergency kit. Both girls were exhausted and settled down to sleep when the pain lessened enough to stop Karina's yelling and crying.

Shortly after eleven o'clock, the fever began. Karina was expecting it, but that didn't provide any comfort. Rattlesnake venom is hematoxic, destroying red blood cells and tissue. Infections are a natural result. Bouncing up and down on the water didn't help. Sipping water relieved the cottony feeling in her mouth, but the vomiting dehydrated her, causing a terrible headache. She prayed the storm would end before morning.

One thing she wasn't sure about—couldn't remember—was whether or not the plane could handle the combined weight of the two girls cradled together in the front seat. Certainly they couldn't weigh more than Martin. She'd flown Martin dozens of times, but that was when she was well, able to fully control both rudder pedals.

She tried to stretch out her leg and place it onto the rudder pedal. Severe pain forced her to back off and the world grew dark. In that half-conscious state, the nightmare came to her. Only this time, she couldn't wake up and make it go away. This time, the nightmare was reality.

Chills started around two o'clock in the morning. Her teeth began chattering, and her head pounded to the rhythm. It got so bad that Tina woke up and worked her way to Karina. Once again, the little girl opened the canopy door. Miraculously, the rain had stopped and the wind had died down.

"Karina, are you cold?"

Karina heard Tina's worried voice from a great distance.

"Here, these may help." The little girl slipped off her denim shorts and tucked them around Karina's neck. Then, she slid next to Karina's good left side as carefully as possible.

Karina was grateful for this extraordinary gesture, but couldn't answer. Her teeth kept chattering, while pain pulsated all through her right side. Her stomach was cramping, and once again, dark mist enveloped her, nature's way of dealing with great pain, a natural anesthetic of the mind.

Bright sunshine funneling through patches of cloud awakened Karina in the morning. Somehow, the pain was manageable. Tina's sleeping body was pressed snugly against her left side. Her warmth was comforting, reassuring. Karina realized that she hadn't even asked the girls how they had come to be alone on that rooftop.

"Wake up, Tina." She gently nudged the child. "We've got to go now, while the pain isn't so bad."

Tina awakened easily, slipped into her shorts, and moved to the front seat to prepare her sister for the flight. Every small movement sickened Karina, and she made frequent use of the barf bags.

"Ready?" she asked the girls after starting the engine. She showed Tina how to adjust the other headset and use the intercom. "Can you hear me?"

"Yes. Are we leaving now?" Tina called back louder than necessary with the electronically assisted microphone. "Can you fly?"

"Yes, we're leaving," replied Karina, turning the ultralight into the wind. "I think I can fly. We have to do something while weather permits."

Karina's takeoff was far from perfect, but she got them into the air. The pain increased with each movement and every adjustment of the rudder. She prayed over and over again for strength to make it to base camp. Flying across the broken sky was bumpy, and each bump became a torment unto itself.

Tina seemed to understand this and tried to help Karina by keeping up a steady chatter. She explained that they had gotten separated from their grandparents a couple of days earlier. Their grandfather's farm had been in danger of being isolated, and they were trying to leave when water pushed the truck off the road. The girls had seen their grandfather help their grandmother to safety, but she and Kelly had been swept away on top of a huge wooden chest that was with them in the back of the truck. They floated on it for hours before coming to land.

They had walked to the house where Karina found them. Only it wasn't flooded at the time. The water started rising later that day, and by nightfall, they had to climb onto the roof. The snakes weren't a problem until the water level got high enough for them to slither out of the water.

Tina had carried food and water to the roof, along with blankets from one of the beds. If Karina hadn't come, Tina was sure the snakes would have gotten them. Twice, large rattlesnakes had made it onto the roof. They got the first one off by throwing their water bottles and food cans at it. The second snake that made it onto the roof, she and Kelly had covered with a blanket and shoved it into the water. Then, they got the idea to snap blankets at the snakes before they could get started, but it was tiring and would have been impossible in the dark.

Talking helped Karina keep her mind off of the excruciating pain in her leg. Every time she moved the rudder, pain made her dizzy, which led to a zigzag course across the sky. She also had trouble maintaining her altitude and a correct heading.

"We should be about there," Karina said to the girls. "See anything?"

"Nothing, but water and islands of trees," Tina said.

Secretly, Karina was worried. Flying the way she was, she couldn't be sure exactly where they were. She used the radio every few minutes with no luck. Now the sky was darkening again, and the wind was picking up. She couldn't control the plane much longer. Her mind could not make sense out of the GPS. Difficult mental tasks seemed beyond her.

A short time later, Karina experienced a terrible muscle spasm in her leg causing the searing pain to burn throughout her entire body. Then, the tears began. She tried hard to keep from crying, but she couldn't help it. The girls encouraged her, cheered her onward, but it didn't help much.

She had just decided to set the plane down near the first solid stretch of dry land she could find, when a familiar voice reached across the distance and asked her to look over her left shoulder. She turned and saw the most beautiful sight in the whole world: Joe in *Meadow Lark*.

"Hey, girl," he said. "I see you've got friends. Where've you been? Everyone's worried sick, and Sally's fit to be tied. She's had us up looking as soon as we had a window of opportunity, and Martin's searching for you. He didn't find anything at the coordinates you gave Sally, yesterday. Over."

She radioed Joe back, and between tears, explained everything that had occurred during her unapproved rescue attempt. Joe informed her she was way off course and was lucky he had seen her when he did. She wasn't far from the landing field, but she was headed in the wrong direction. If he hadn't come along, she would have missed it altogether.

Karina's radio wasn't working very well, and Joe had trouble understanding her. When she switched to their alternate frequency, reception improved.

"Joe," she said, switching off Tina's headset so the little girl couldn't listen in on their conversation. "I don't think I can make it. I've got to set down now, or I'm going to black out and crash. Over."

"We're only five minutes out," Joe said. "I've alerted everyone of your situation. They're all waiting for you. You're a hero, kid. You've got to make it. For me. Besides, after what those two little girls have faced so bravely, you owe it to them to finish. Just stay on my wing and follow me in. Over."

"I'll try. Over," she said. Tears prevented her from saying more.

After that, things rapidly worsened. The air became choppy, the wind increased and pain finally got the best of Karina. During one prolonged, excruciating pain, she jerked on the control stick, pulled the plane's nose too high, and stalled. The stall made her dizzy and disoriented. She lost almost a thousand feet of altitude before she regained control. In the front seat, the two girls were absolutely quiet, terrorized with fear.

Joe tried hard to help her. "Karina, lower your left wing. Karina, put your nose down. Come on, the runway's in sight. You can make it. Over."

"Sorry," Karina whispered into her microphone. She wasn't sure to whom she was apologizing; maybe to the girls, maybe to Joe, or perhaps to Martin.

"Penny?" her friend's image appeared through her torment. Karina tried to picture the energetic little figure in her mind, but couldn't stay focused. "Joe, I'm scared. I'm not going to make it."

She never heard his response. Her ultralight descended in the general direction of the runway. Vaguely, she heard Tina yell. Fear had its grip on her now, but even that didn't matter. The pain was so intense at that moment. Karina just wanted it to end, to drift into that world where darkness replaced both fear and pain. She had given up. Now, whatever happened would just have to happen. Her hand went slack on the control stick, and the ultralight nosed sharply downward.

"*Don't worry, darling. Everything will be all right in its own time.*" The familiar words filled her mind, eclipsing all other thought.

"Mother?" Karina pulled on the stick with her last ounce of strength.

The little plane had been diving straight for the ground. Karina's backward pressure lifted its nose upward. Her airspeed slowed as the attitude increased, and the plane stalled about ten feet above the ground. It hit hard, bending both wheel struts outward, then bounced high into the air and spiraled into the ground. Karina no longer felt pain, nor did she hear the frightened screams in front of her. Darkness engulfed the entire world. Her mother's voice radiated all around her, encompassing her as snugly as a mother's comforting arms.

Chapter 12

▼

The Final Struggle

"Karina. Karina. Open your eyes. Come on, you can do it," said a strong familiar voice.

The fog lifted a little. Karina opened her eyes and looked into Martin's somber expression. "Where am I? What happened?" She tried to move, but couldn't.

"You're in a hospital in Albuquerque." Martin spoke slowly, carefully pronouncing each word. "You crashed after being bitten by a rattlesnake, remember?"

Karina closed her eyes for a long moment. "The girls?"

"They're okay," Martin said. He took hold of Karina's hand. "Tina broke her arm trying to protect her sister, but she's all right. Both girls have been reunited with their grandparents. You saved their lives, kiddo. We're proud of you."

She had a terrible headache. "Martin, I can't move. What's wrong with me? Is my back broken? My neck?"

"No, nothing like that. You've been restrained because you were having convulsive muscle spasms." Martin patted her hand. "Are you awake enough to talk? We really need to talk."

Karina came slowly out of the fog. She had pain, but it wasn't too bad. From the corner of her eye, she saw that she was connected to an IV machine. Its steady drip told her she was being filled with something. "Sure. I'm sorry about the plane. I know I'm grounded. It's okay."

"I wish it was that simple." Martin paused.

He was having trouble telling her something. Of that, she was sure. "What is it?" she asked. "Just tell me. I'm getting a little dizzy."

"Karina, the doctors want to amputate your right leg, just below the hip." Martin tightened his grip on Karina's hand. "They say you will probably die if they don't operate soon. You've been here a week already, and your leg isn't responding well to treatment. Too large a snake, too much venom."

From deep inside, Karina started to cry. She begged Martin not to let them amputate her leg. She would rather die. "Why did you bring me back, anyway?" she asked. "I was with my mother. Please don't let them. Please!"

* * *

She walked through fields of flowers, hearing every sweet sound of nature. A cool breeze blew lightly through her hair. Sunlight filled a cloudless sky. Friends seemed to be all around, but Karina couldn't see them. They were just voices sailing on the air, resting here, resting there, never staying in one place for long. The pain and torment were gone. She didn't understand why she had been so frightened. Nothing here could harm her. She could run with the wind and never tire.

* * *

"Mommy, I think her eyelids moved." The hopeful voice seemed closer than the others.

Karina searched, but couldn't quite locate the voice. It seemed to be right on top of her, but she couldn't find the source.

"Keep talking, dear," said another familiar voice. "She's trying to come out of it. Keep talking."

Finally, Karina's eyes opened and she blinked at the unaccustomed light. "Penny? Is that you?" Karina looked into bright blue eyes. Was she still in New Mexico? "Where are we?"

"Hi, Karina." Penny jumped up and down. Tears streamed from her eyes and rolled down her cheeks. "Mommy, she's awake. She's awake. Get the doctor, quick."

"Hi." Karina reached out and patted Penny to make sure the child was real. "Don't cry. You'll be okay. The doctor said your transplant was successful."

Penny smiled, wiping joyous tears away with her forearm. "I'm fine. I was so worried about you. You've been out for so long. They didn't know whether or not you'd wake up again."

"How long?" she asked, dimly aware there was something she really wanted—no, needed—to know."

"Penny, go outside and tell Daddy that Karina is awake," Mrs. Winfield said.

Karina suddenly remembered what was so important. "My leg?" she asked.

"You still have your leg," Mrs. Winfield said. "Martin wouldn't let the doctors amputate. He followed your request and even got a court order to prevent it. We're so happy to have you back with us. It's been almost three weeks."

"What about the flood? Blue Horizons? Joe, and the kids?" Karina felt as if the world had passed her by.

Mrs. Winfield filled in the blanks. "The weather pattern has changed, and the worst of the flooding is over. You have been in and out of consciousness for almost three weeks."

"What about Martin and the kids?" Karina asked again.

"Martin and the Blue Horizons group are almost finished with the cross-country flight. Martin calls three times a day to check on your progress. You really had us worried, honey." Mrs. Winfield adjusted the bed so Karina could see more. "Now, you're going to be fine, but there are still some tough times ahead."

"Tough times? What do you mean?" Karina voiced her question in such a low voice that she wasn't even sure that she had spoken.

Mrs. Winfield patted Karina's shoulder. "Karina, you are going to need extensive physical therapy before you'll be able to walk normally. We have arranged with Martin to take you home with us as soon as the doctors give the okay. Would you like that?"

"Yes, certainly," she said. But tears came anyway. Karina ignored the fact that she had saved at least three lives from the vicious flood. Self-pity took control. She felt a total failure. She couldn't follow orders. She'd crashed the ultralight. Everyone had finished the journey except her.

Mrs. Winfield held her until she fell asleep again, gently rocking her, urging her to cry it all out. She soothed Karina by repeating over and over again how happy everyone was that she was getting better.

* * *

Three days later, during one of her depressed moods, Karina had another visitor. Penny had been chased out. For a moment, she thought the little imp had sneaked back into the room. Then, she noticed Mr. Smithson standing inside the door.

"I heard you had a bad day in therapy," he said. "How are you doing?"

"I'm not a cripple, if that's what you mean," she answered crossly. "But I'm not much good for anything, either. I guess you're here to tell me I'm through at Blue Horizons. If you are, it's okay. I won't argue. I don't deserve to be there anyway."

"I thought you liked Blue Horizons," the little man said. "I certainly hope you do because I've got a proposition for you. That is, if you want it."

"What proposition?" Karina asked suspiciously. She never knew exactly what to make of Mr. Smithson.

He pulled up a chair and sat by her bed. "Well, it seems I need another group of dedicated pilots ready to take on a challenge. Think you're up to a challenge?"

"Maybe, what is it?" she asked. He certainly had her attention.

"I've been asked by a biological foundation if we might provide some pilots and ultralights to do aerial photography. It'll be a tough job, but the scenery will be beautiful. Joe's already agreed, as have Jessica and Paul. We need a fourth, besides Martin, Sally, and myself, of course. Want to be part of the team?"

Karina felt her heart skipping beats. "I'm not going to be much good for a long time. When will we have to leave? Where are we going?"

Mr. Smithson smiled. "You've got a little time. We don't leave until the end of December. It takes some training to fly over the Amazon rain forest."

Did she hear him right, the Amazon? Could this be real? she wondered. "You mean like in South America?"

Mr. Smithson assured her that the job was real. Everyone had voted to include her in the project. The only catch had been that she'd have to work hard on both her physical therapy and Spanish.

"Think it over," Mr. Smithson said. "I don't want an answer now. I'll be back at the conclusion of the cross-country flight, in about another week. Tell me then." He departed after delivering a huge pile of get-well letters from her classmates.

For more than an hour after Mr. Smithson's departure, Karina reflected on the many turns her life had taken over the past five months. She had come to Blue Horizons an angry, spoiled child. What was she now? She felt she had grown. Certainly, she wasn't as angry as before. Her nightmares no longer dominated her existence, even though they had not fully departed.

She had also made friends with the kids of Blue Horizons, and considered Jessica a sister. She even had a boyfriend, of sorts. Joe had saved her life. If he hadn't been there when she needed him, she wouldn't be here now. That thought brought a snug, comforting glow, warming her from within, easing the painful muscle cramps that currently demanded her attention.

She rubbed her leg and thought about Penny and the Winfields. If she hadn't been sent to Blue Horizons, she might never have found another family. Yes, family. The Winfields were more family than she'd had in years. Her aunt and uncle had provided her a home, but they had never taken the time to understand her.

On top of it all, she had even secured Martin's interest. She now realized just how much she had come to respect Martin. He had become her surrogate father. Even when he was angry or disappointed in her, Martin didn't give up. Perhaps with such guidance, she could grow up to be somebody others might like. Maybe she could even begin to like herself.

Karina didn't need to think about Mr. Smithson's offer for long. If they were willing to have her, she was willing to go. Her mood greatly improved with thoughts of all the blessings that had been bestowed upon her during her time at Blue Horizons and the possibility of more challenges ahead. Karina sent Penny to get her real food: hamburgers.

When the child returned and handed her the aromatic bag, Karina thanked her emphatically. "Gracious, mi amiga." She dug into hamburgers and french fries, and wondered what kind of food people ate in a rain forest.

Afterword

Many of the events in *Across a Broken Sky* are real-life situations. In true life, Karina is not one person, but the combination of many adolescent students. The person depicted as Karina came from a country called Kyrgyzstan, and helped build and fly an ultralight airplane. Other scenes of helping with the flood, being bitten by a venomous snake, and bargaining for a spanking over another form of punishment are all real situations that have been called upon to bring Karina to life. Follow Karina as she portrays the essence of growing up. But, one must remember that in real life, happy endings are never a certainty.

Karina learned much about herself during that long eventful flight across the United States. She learned to look past herself and to place others first. Her selfless acts in caring for Penny, saving the helicopter crew, and rescuing the two children show promise for the future. However, the troubled fourteen-year-old has not yet fully dealt with the anger within her, or learned other necessary lessons about life. Like most teens, Karina wants to be in control, to choose her own direction, to make her own decisions.

Leaving the hospital to rest and recover with Penny and her parents will be a great benefit, but future problems lie in store. There is danger in the impetuousness of youth. Follow Karina's next excursion, which leads her into the Amazon rain forest and new adventures that give her further insights about growing up. In *Beyond Tears: The Point of No Return*, Karina will have to cross that adolescent bridge into adulthood, making decisions that will forever affect the lives of those she meets.

About the Author

Terry Umphenour is a respected science teacher who leads middle school students in search of their own talents and identities. He has taken students on research projects into the Amazon Rainforest, the ocean's depths, up mountains, and into the realm of flight. The Karina series is based upon those adventures.

0-595-17949-5